ONE EXTRA SPARKLE

Ellie and the Marriage List

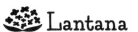 Lantana

First published in the United Kingdom in 2024 by Lantana Publishing Ltd.
Clavier House, 21 Fifth Road, Newbury RG14 6DN, UK
www.lantanapublishing.com | info@lantanapublishing.com

American edition published in 2024 by Lantana Publishing Ltd., UK.

Text © Tricia Seabolt, 2024
Illustration © Lucy Rogers, 2024

Distributed in the United States and Canada by Lerner Publishing Group, Inc.
241 First Avenue North, Minneapolis, MN 55401 U.S.A.
For reading levels and more, look for this title at www.lernerbooks.com
Cataloging-in-Publication Data Available.

Hardcover ISBN: 978-1-915244-72-7
ePDF ISBN: 978-1-915244-73-4
ePub3 S&L ISBN: 978-1-915244-75-8
ePub3 Trade ISBN: 978-1-915244-74-1

Printed and bound in China using plant-based inks on
sustainably sourced paper.

To my parents for keeping my childhood bookshelves full, and in memory of my grandparents who always cheered me on.

—Tricia

To my lovely family: Mum, Dad and little brother, Henry, who is not so little anymore. I had so many wonderful memories growing up with you all.

—Lucy

ONE EXTRA SPARKLE

Ellie and the Marriage List

Tricia Seabolt Lucy Rogers

Chapter 1

Ellie clunked down the hallway in her lucky T-shirt and hiking boots.

Clunk, clunk, clunk!

It felt good to make such big noises after waiting for her brother all morning.

Clunk, clunk, clunk!

With each clunk, her brownish ponytail bobbed, and her glasses slid further down her nose. With each clunk, she remembered all the times she'd had to wait for Ben this summer.

Ellie pressed her ear against the bathroom door and listened. "Yes!" she squealed. *Finally! No more shower sounds!*

"Ben!" Ellie called. "Are you ready *now*?"

"Ready for what?" Ben replied in his teasing voice.

"*You know!*" Usually, Ellie liked joking with her brother. But why did he have to take a super-long shower *before* their special hike? Ben used to take her hiking in the woods behind their neighborhood a lot. Had he forgotten about the messy parts? What about the rabbit poop and watermelon-sized spider webs?

At least Mom had agreed with her. "Showering after the hike would make more sense," she'd said. "You two come back from those woods smelling worse than a basket of Ben's sweaty soccer socks!"

Dad had tried to cheer Ellie up before he'd left for the office. "Teenagers do funny things sometimes. When I was fifteen like Ben, my buddies and I had a contest to see who could go the longest without showering!" He said he'd made it five days before Grandma had told him he'd sleep outside if he didn't wash the stench off.

Chapter 1

Ellie had giggled a little at that part. But she hadn't let herself get too cheered up. Besides, she didn't think the teenager things Ben did were funny *at all*. In fact, they made her want to stay ten years old forever. The captain-of-the-soccer-team thing and his job-stocking-shelves-at-Albert's-Convenience-Store thing were especially terrible. Between these two very *not-funny* things, Ben was never home. Sometimes, Ellie wondered if he even remembered he had a little sister.

"Can you check the hiking backpack for me, El?" Ben called. "Make sure I packed the essentials – you know, cheesy chips and mini donuts!"

"I did!" Ellie shoved her bangs off her forehead. She'd checked the backpack lots of times already. She loved how Ben had remembered her favorite snacks and her *Guide to Forest Animals* book. But they would never get to enjoy them if he didn't hurry!

Clatter, clatter, clatter.

What was Ben doing in there? Ellie scanned the

photographs lining the walls because they were more interesting than the bathroom door. Her favorite was the one of Dad pulling a dollar out of Grandma's ear at the family reunion. It made Ellie excited for when he finally got the real magician job he'd been dreaming of for so long. Then he wouldn't have to go to that boring office ever again!

Clatter, clatter, clatter.

Her eyes landed on a photograph of Ben as a little kid. He had a missing-tooth smile and was waving from the window of the backyard treehouse. That was before he'd outgrown it. And before the treehouse had turned haunted.

Nobody believed Ellie and her best friend,

Chapter 1

Ling, about the haunted part. But both girls knew what they'd seen during the spookiest sleepover ever. A sleepover so terrifying, they'd made a vow to never ever set foot in the treehouse.

"Let's look for a fox!" Ellie called, hugging her nature notebook. The cover was plastered with bug stickers and *Ellie Anderson, Wildlife Artist* was scrawled in the corner. She'd been carrying it around all morning, imagining the pointy-nosed creature she'd draw inside.

"Don't foxes usually hide during the day?" Ben replied between the sound of drawers and cupboards opening and shutting. "How about a rabbit?"

"I have two rabbit pictures!" Maybe Ben had forgotten about that too. After all, he barely had time to look at her nature notebook anymore.

"Well, if anyone could track down a fox in broad daylight, it would be my sister!" Ben said. "Are you wearing your all-mighty lucky T-shirt?"

"Yep!" Ellie replied. If Ben would only open the door, he could see for himself. She saved her lucky T-shirt for hikes. Only hikes! It helped her find the coolest animals in the whole forest. Not only was it green, her favorite color, but it also said *Down Syndrome is my Superpower!* in glittery letters.

"Maybe it can help me find a great white shark!" Ben called. "That would be epic!"

"*Bennnnn!*" Ellie reminded him they weren't going on an ocean hike as she patted the pocket of her jean shorts. *Good!* The fresh tube of orange, fox-colored paint was still there.

Usually, she liked sketching with her triangle pencil because it had three flat sides to help her grip when her fingers got as tired and floppy as spaghetti noodles. But special occasions like hikes with

Chapter 1

her brother were perfect for using paint from the grown-up artist set she'd gotten for her birthday.

"I'm almost done!" Ben said. "I'll meet you under the weeping willow, okay?"

The weeping willow was the backyard tree she drew under every day—the same one that held the haunted tree house. Once, Dad had told her that *weeping* meant crying. Ellie didn't blame her weeping willow one bit for being sad. After all, it had to carry something super creepy in its branches.

"Okay, El?" Ben prompted from behind the bathroom door.

"*Okay!*" Ellie grumbled. Then she clunked back down the hall, wishing her lucky T-shirt had the power to make her brother hurry up.

Clunk! Clunk! Clunk!

Chapter 2

Haunted treehouse or not, the weeping willow
was the one thing that could make Ellie forget her
angry-at-Ben-for-taking-a-shower-on-the-best-day-
of-summer feelings. Nature notebook in hand, she
marched across the backyard, following the branches
that twisted above her like wild octopuses' arms.

"Hey, Ellie!"

She'd almost made it to her favorite drawing spot
when she heard Ling calling. "Hey!" Ellie waved. Her
best friend stood on her side of the raspberry-bush-
covered fence in a long, grape-colored sundress. Ling
wore dresses every day because she was practicing
for when she became a movie star.

Chapter 2

"Sorry I can't come over today." Ling adjusted her sparkly-rimmed sunglasses as Ellie joined her at the fence. "But please ask me why! It's the best reason in the whole history of the world!"

"Why?" Ellie glanced over her shoulder at the far corner of her yard. She always drew on the same side of the giant weeping willow trunk. The side *without* the haunted tree house.

"Mom's taking me to Dance World after my piano lesson!"

Ling twirled in the grass, her long black hair floating behind her. "She's buying me a plush pink leotard!"

"You *have* pink ones!" Ellie reminded her. It was true. Ling had a whole drawerful of pink leotards.

"Those are *regular* pink," Ling said. "Regular pink leotards are too babyish now that I'm ten and a half. And none of the girls in my ballet class have a plush pink one yet. Not even Sophia!"

Sophia was Ling's BBF which meant *Best Ballet*

Ellie and the Marriage List

Friend. But Ellie was Ling's BFF which meant *Best Friend Forever*. Ling said BFFs were the most important kind because you never stopped being best friends, even when you were old, wrinkly grandmas.

"Ling!" shrieked Zhi from the back door. "Did you drink all the orange juice?"

Chapter 2

Ling flashed Ellie a smile before calling back, "Yep!"

"You're a brat! I barely got any!" Zhi slammed the door.

Zhi was Ling's older sister. She was in high school, but Ling said she acted like she was in preschool.

"She deserved it!" Ling told Ellie with a shrug. "She and Eddy hogged it all last time."

Eddy was Zhi's boyfriend. He had tattoos and drove a rattly car covered in bumper stickers.

"Was she sorry?" Ellie fanned herself with her nature notebook. It was so hot that the raspberry bushes smelled like fruity pie baking in the sun.

"Nope!" Ling poked out her chin. "And yesterday she used my glitter-glamour nail polish without permission! Now I barely have enough for my pinky fingers!"

Ellie's own fingers ached to sketch whiskers and bushy tails. Drawing was how she forgot Ben problems, like Dance World was how Ling forgot Zhi problems.

"How come you're so quiet?" Ling asked.

Ellie wanted to tell Ling about Ben. But it made her mouth hurt to even think about the words. Instead, she glanced back at her weeping willow, waiting for her like a dinosaur-sized shaggy dog. Luckily, from this angle, the haunted treehouse was almost invisible beneath the thick leaves and branches. But the rope ladder leading up, and the yellow-as-a-lemon slide going down, were impossible to miss.

"Oh! I forgot to tell you the best part!" Ling said when Ellie still didn't speak. "Dance World's website says I'll look like a blooming rose when I dance in a plush pink leotard!"

Imagining her BFF as a giant flower made Ellie giggle. It felt good to laugh after such a grumpy morning. Behind her, the bird rock band joined in, singing a happy tune from their stage in the tip-top branches of her tree.

Chapter 2

"Hey!" Ling crossed her arms as Ellie's giggles got louder. "Shouldn't you be hiking with Ben right now?"

And just like that, all her laughs dried up. Ellie's shoulders slumped as she stared across the yard at the closed-tight back door.

"Ellie?" Ling prompted. "Are you okay?"

"Ben's a slowpoke!" Ellie grumbled.

"Why? What's he doing?" Ling asked. "I thought he had the day off from Albert's and soccer."

"He's... He's...in the..." It wasn't only Ellie's fingers that got the spaghetti noodle feeling. Other parts of her did too. Even her talking muscles. Not only did it make saying big words hard, but it also made saying little words when she was full of big feelings hard too.

"He's in the *where?*" Ling prompted.

"Shower!" The word burst out of her mouth sounding more like *showa.* 'R' wasn't an easy sound to make, and the thought of Ben shampooing his hair instead of hiking with her made it even harder to get right.

Ling wrinkled her nose. "But he'll get all gross in the woods anyway."

"I know," whispered Ellie.

"I have an idea!" Ling cried. "Come to Dance World with me instead!"

Ellie shook her head so hard her ponytail whipped her cheeks. "I need to wait for Ben!"

"You don't need Ben for *everything* anymore," Ling said. "Soon you'll be ten and a half like me. And that's almost a teenager!"

Before Ellie could say she never wanted to be a teenager and that she'd always need Ben, Ling screeched, "Here he comes now! But what's up with his hair?"

Ellie spun around to see her brother striding towards them with the hiking backpack. She gasped. Ling was right! Usually, Ben's brownish hair was a little messy like hers. But today it was stuck in one place like a giant bike helmet!

"It's glue!" Ellie screeched. Ben would be in so much trouble when Mom and Dad found out!

"Nope," Ling said as Ben got closer. "It's gel. Eddy plasters that same stuff in his hair when he and Zhi go on dates."

Then Mr. Yang called Ling in for her piano lesson. With a promise to hula hoop the next day, she took off towards her house.

But Ellie barely noticed. She was too busy wondering how many foxes Ben's hair would scare away.

Chapter 3

"Are you okay?" Ben asked as they headed through the backyard gate.

Ellie stumbled along next to her brother with his frozen-in-one-place hair. Up close, in the bright, sunny front yard, it was worse than she'd thought. Much worse. "Your hair!" she managed.

"What's wrong with it?" Ben asked, as if it didn't look like he was wearing a helmet of spiky caterpillars.

But before Ellie could speak, Sara McMillon from across the street showed up in jean shorts, a light blue T-shirt, and loads of lip gloss. She was fifteen like Ben and had lots of cupcake-sprinkle freckles.

Chapter 3

Ellie had always wanted a friend with freckles. But ever since Sara moved from Arizona at the beginning of the summer, she'd been more of Ben's friend than hers.

"Hey, guys!" Sara tucked her short, butter-noodle-colored hair behind her ear.

"What's up?" Ben grinned so big at Sara that it looked like his face would split in half.

"Not much." Sara tipped her chin up to gaze at Ben with his tall, skyscraper hair. "What's up with you?"

"Ben has hair jelly!" Ellie blurted, proud that she remembered the name Ling had told her.

Sarah's eyebrows shot up. "Hair jelly?"

"It's not jelly, El," muttered Ben as they started down the sidewalk together.

"Yes, it is!" Ellie insisted.

"No! It's just a little hair gel." For some reason, her brother's face was getting redder by the second.

Just then, the Yang's garage opened, and their car

backed down the driveway. Ling's frowning face was pressed against the passenger window. Ellie tried to wave, but her BFF seemed to be watching Sara and Ben instead. As Mrs. Yang zoomed past, Ellie wondered why Ling looked sad when she was on her way to Dance World.

"Hopefully it's *strawberry* jelly," Sara said to Ellie a moment later. "I'll take strawberry over grape any day!"

"Me too!" Ellie liked how Sara never forgot to talk to her like some of her brother's friends. Like Ben, Sara worked around the block at Albert's Convenience Store, and lately she'd been riding her bike to the park to watch him play soccer. And sometimes, while Ellie was getting ready for bed, she saw them talking under her tree.

Ellie's heart thumped with excitement when they came to the place where their street dead-ended. Beyond stretched the crunchy field of dried-up weeds she and Ben had tromped through time after

Chapter 3

time to get to the forest clearing.

Finally. Finally, it was time for Sara to walk back to her house. Then, Ellie and Ben could start hiking and searching for foxes.

"Bye, Sara!" Ellie waved. She waited for her brother to do the same. But Ben wasn't waving to Sara, and Sara wasn't walking back to her house.

Ellie tried again. "See you later, Sara!" Maybe they could stop at the McMillons' on their way home and show Sara her fox picture.

"Hold on, El," Ben said. "Sara and I have a surprise for you."

Ellie spun around because the word *surprise* tickled her ears the same way *Christmas* and *ice cream* did. "What? What is it?"

Sara smiled at Ben, then at Ellie, before speaking. "I'm coming hiking with you guys!"

The giant grin on Ben's face was growing by the second. "You've been wanting to hang out with Sara, right, El?"

Ellie nodded, but no words would come.

"I've wanted to hang out with you too, Ellie," Sara said softly.

Ellie hugged her nature notebook. She wanted Sara to be her friend. But she didn't want her to go on their brother-sister hike! She didn't want *anyone* to go except her and Ben!

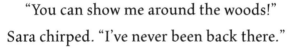

"You can show me around the woods!" Sara chirped. "I've never been back there."

"My sister can navigate those trails with her eyes closed," Ben joked. Then he squeezed Ellie's shoulders. "What do you say? Totally your call."

Ellie's mouth hung open as she looked at them.

"If...umm...you don't want me to come, I totally get it..." Sara's voice trailed off.

"I bet El wants you to come," Ben prompted. "Right, El?"

Sara's freckles disappeared beneath the pink in her cheeks when Ellie remained silent. "Maybe I should just go home."

"No!" Ben shouted. Then he lowered his voice as he met Ellie's eyes. "I mean, wait a sec. Come on, El. Is it cool for Sara to hike with us?"

Ellie couldn't stand disappointing her brother. Not when he looked so hopeful. So she took a deep breath before marching ahead into the crispy field.

"Okay," she called over her shoulder. "You can come."

Chapter 4

The trio crunched through the sunburned field toward the clearing. But the sun wasn't out now. Maybe *it* didn't like how the best day of summer was turning out either.

"Hey, Ellie," Sara said. "Did I tell you I had a treehouse when I lived in Arizona?"

Ben coughed a little. "Ellie doesn't play in our treehouse."

"Why?" Sara asked. "I played in mine all the time when I was younger!"

"It's haunted!" Ellie whispered as a familiar fear tiptoed up her spine.

"Did you say your treehouse is haunted?" Sara

side-stepped closer to Ben.

"Yep!" Ellie's head bobbed as they neared the clearing. "She dances too!"

"Who dances?" Sara asked.

"You really have to drop this whole ballerina ghost thing, El." Ben shook his head.

"Ballerina ghost?" Sara croaked. "Really?"

"Not really," Ben laughed. "I played up there every single day when I was Ellie's age, and the scariest thing I saw was some squirrel poop."

But Sara was still looking at Ellie. "How many times have you seen her?"

Ellie held up one finger. Once was more than enough. Besides, after the vow they'd made to never set foot in the treehouse, she and Ling had promised to *never ever* look at it at night. That was when the ballerina ghost danced, and neither girl wanted to risk another sighting. But no matter how hard Ellie tried or how long ago that sleepover had been, she couldn't push that shivery winter night out of her brain. How could she with the treehouse right there in her backyard, reminding her day after day?

"Ghost stuff majorly freaks me out!" Sara edged even closer to Ben who puffed out his chest like Superman.

"Me too," Ellie admitted because too much ballerina ghost talk made her words stick together—like she was chewing on a spiderweb.

"Perfect time to change the subject." Ben gave the sleeve of Ellie's lucky T-shirt a tug. "Tell Sara what animal to watch for!"

The grumpy part of Ellie wanted to keep her plan for a fox portrait a secret. But the bigger part of her—the part that wanted to be Sara's friend—was desperate to tell her all about it.

"How about a clue, Ellie?" Sara asked as a warm breeze rolled across the papery weeds only to be gobbled up by the trees ahead. "What does it look like?"

"It has sharp teeth," Ellie replied. "And claws."

Chapter 4

"Seriously?" Sara asked as they faced each other in the clearing. "It's not a bear, right?"

"Come on, El." Ben passed out water from the backpack. "Spill the beans!"

Ben had told her that *Spill the beans* meant you were about to say something important. And Ellie liked saying important things.

"Tell me, Ellie!" Sara said. "I'm dying to know what you're going to draw!"

"A fox!" As Ellie made the announcement, she longed to squeeze that fat tube of grown-up artist paint and watch it curl onto the page of her nature notebook like orange toothpaste.

"Cool!" Sara said. "But umm, are they dangerous?"

Ellie shook her head, excited to reveal one of the coolest facts from her *Guide to Forest Animals* book. "They eat worms!" Of course they ate other stuff too, but worms were the most interesting.

Ellie and the Marriage List

As they made their way deeper into the forest, Sara asked, "But what if you can't find a fox?"

"My lucky T-shirt helps!" Ellie told her.

"You should see this thing in action!" Ben said. "Deer, massive spiders, even my buddy's lost dog last summer. I wouldn't be surprised if she tracks down a gorilla one day!"

When Ben stopped to collect the empty water bottles a little later, Sara pointed at Ellie's hand. "Whoa! Your ring is practically glowing!"

 At the mention of her extra sparkle ring, Ellie smiled. It was her birthday gift from Mom, Dad, and Ben. Sara was right. Even in the shadowy forest, it shimmered like grass, glittery with raindrops.

"Dad got it out of his ma...ma...ma...magician hat." She could still hear his voice while her friends at the party cheered. *Ta da! An extra sparkle for our*

Chapter 4

girl with the extra sparkle!

"What did you say?" Sara dipped her head close to Ellie's.

Magician was a big *and* exciting word, so it was especially difficult. Ellie tried again because she was used to saying things over and over. Especially to people who didn't know her as well as her family and Ling did.

"I'm sorry." Sara's eyes flicked to Ben. "I still don't understand."

Since Ellie's tongue sometimes got stuck on big words like *magician,* Maria, her speech therapist, taught her exercises to help. Plus, she gave Ellie cool bug stickers for the cover of her nature notebook. But today, with Sara taking over their hike, Ellie couldn't remember a single tongue-unsticking trick Maria had taught her.

"Dad's magician hat," Ben jumped in to help. "He got El's extra sparkle ring out of his magician hat."

"Why is it called an extra sparkle ring?" asked

Sara.

"So Ellie always remembers how *extra* cool she is." Ben gave Ellie a wink before telling Sara the part about chromosomes. About how Ellie had one extra chromosome than kids who didn't have Down syndrome.

Chromosome was an even more tongue-twisty word than magician, so Ellie was happy to let Ben tell Sara. Besides, chromosomes were way more boring than finding foxes.

It got darker and darker as they made their way further into the tunnel of trees. "Is it night, Ben?" Ellie demanded. Maybe all of that waiting for her brother had wasted her best day of summer!

Ben glanced at his cell phone. "It's barely one o'clock in the afternoon, El."

But Ellie couldn't remember the forest ever being *this* dark. With the trees casting shadows as thick and billowy as smoke, it was no wonder she hadn't found a fox yet! That, or Ben's hair was freaking

Chapter 4

them all out.

"It's those massive clouds rolling in." Ben squinted up at the forest ceiling.

And that's when the first raindrops hit.

"My nature notebook!" Ellie tried to shield it with her body, but Ben grabbed it and tossed it into the backpack.

The rain came faster and faster, pelting the leaves above like popcorn. Now Ben's stuck-in-one-place hair looked like melted chocolate dripping down his forehead.

Sara slipped the backpack on her shoulders as Ben stooped down. "Hop on, El!" Ellie jumped on his back like when she was little. She held on tight, bouncing along like a baby monkey as Ben sprinted down the splashy, muddy path, through the clearing and across the now soggy field.

By the time Ben's sneakers slapped the sidewalk of their neighborhood a few moments later, Ellie was starting to slip. *Was she getting too big? Ben used to be* strong enough to hold her!

"I'm falling!" Ellie screamed as she inched closer to the sloshy puddles below.

"I've got you, El!" Ben yelled back. But it didn't feel like he had her.

It didn't feel like her brother had her at all.

Then a firework-sized flash of lightning lit up the neighborhood. And suddenly Ellie could see. Even through her smudged-as-rainy-windshields glasses, she could see.

She wasn't falling because she was too big.

She was falling because Ben was holding Sara's hand.

Chapter 5

After they dropped Sara off, the storm raged on all evening. From the kitchen window, Ellie watched her weeping willow rock back and forth like it was boxing with the wind.

"Has anyone seen my coconut?" Dad asked as he rifled through cabinets.

"Maybe it really disappeared this time, dear!" Mom looked up from the table where she was making sea-animal-shaped name tags for the Ability Center dance.

Ellie loved hanging out with her friends from the Ability Center (or AC for short). They always did cool stuff like movie nights and workout warrior

Chapter 5

classes. But the summer dance was everyone's favorite.

"I can't believe it's only two weeks away!" Mom gave Ellie's hand a squeeze from across the table. "Are you excited?"

"Yes, yes, yes!"

Dad performed a magic show at the dance every year, but this time he said Ellie could help with the grand finale trick. Ben would be the DJ like always, and Mom would help with everything else. Last year, she untangled streamers from the spokes of her friend, Kendra's, wheelchair, rescued a kid's hearing aid from the punch bowl, and fixed Ben's microphone.

There was only one bad thing about this year's dance.

"I'll miss Ling." Ellie sighed. The kids who hung out at the AC always got to invite their family and friends to the dance. Ellie always asked Ling, and Ling always said yes.

Except this time.

"We will too," said Dad as he swung open the fridge to continue the coconut hunt. "Ling has accompanied you to the dance every summer since you started going to the AC."

"But it's important for Ling to support her sister," said Mom gently.

Ellie had that same pokey feeling she got every time she thought about Ling's parents forcing her to watch Zhi's violin solo at the community center concert instead of going to the AC dance.

"You'll still have a blast, honey. I promise!" Mom handed her a tiny catfish name tag. "Here. I need an artist's opinion."

As she admired the tiny whiskers, Ellie gave Mom a thumbs up. She liked it when her family needed her. Mom was a math teacher at a grown-up school called college, so she didn't know very much about art stuff.

My name is Tara, and I'm down to dance! was

scrawled across the catfish's belly. Tara was one of Ellie's best AC friends. She had a purple *Down Syndrome is my Superpower!* T-shirt, and she knew how to make cool mice out of foil for her kitten, Oscar.

"Good news, El!" Ben burst into the kitchen. "Your nature notebook and cheesy chips are safe!"

Ellie grinned. This was the kind of Ben she liked best. No bike helmet hair, soccer uniform, or vest from Albert's. Just a T-shirt, sweatpants, and his regular, messy brother hair.

"Here you are, Madame!" Ben opened the bag of chips and handed it to Ellie along with her nature notebook.

"Thanks, Ben!" Ellie could open her own chips. But they tasted better when he did it.

"Check it out!" Ben settled at the table by the window. "The treehouse looks like it's about to get launched into outer space!"

"Really?"
Ellie was
hopeful
as she took
another look
into her stormy
backyard.
At that
moment, a
flash of lightning
exploded across the
sky, illuminating the
treehouse like a splintery
box of bones.
"I was joking, El!" Ben
laughed. "It's so overgrown
since I played in there, that thing is

practically anchored to the tree now!"

"Well, I hope this crash course in Michigan weather doesn't scare Sara too much," Dad called from inside the fridge.

"I'll text her now to see if she's okay." Ben pulled out his phone.

Ellie crunched on a cheesy chip. "Sara's okay!" Ben had asked her enough times when they'd dropped her off across the street. *Ellie* was the one who wasn't okay. She was the one without a fox in her nature notebook.

"Your father and I are certainly glad the McMillons moved in," Mom said as Ellie scooted closer to Ben. "Sara's parents are just as sweet as she is."

Ellie opened her nature notebook to show her brother how good she'd gotten at drawing skinny grasshopper knees.

"You're right, Mom. She's super chill. Unlike most girls." Ben was so busy talking about Sara and texting Sara that he seemed to forget Ellie was even there.

Ellie wanted to know what *chill* meant. Then maybe she could *chill* too! But she didn't get a chance to ask because at that moment, Dad found his coconut.

"A-ha!" He backed out of the fridge, bonking his head. Then he waved it in the air for his family to see. "Isn't she a beauty?"

"Almost as beautiful as your wife!" Mom fluffed her hair.

"But I love my wife too much to make her disappear!" Dad zipped over to plant a kiss on Mom's head.

Ellie decided that the one good thing about the storm outside was how cozy it felt to be with her family inside.

If only Ben would put his phone down, everything would be perfect.

Chapter 6

The next morning, Ling burst through Ellie's backyard gate with her purple hula hoop and a not-happy face. The same face Ellie had seen pressed against the car window as Mrs. Yang zipped off to Dance World yesterday.

"Are you okay?" Ellie asked as she put the finishing touches on her robin drawing.

"I'm not even a little okay!" Ling twisted the strap of the tiny purse slung over her shoulder. It matched her long, shiny dress. This dress was from her grandma in China and had a fancy name Ellie couldn't remember.

Ling's family had moved to Michigan from China

while she was in Mrs. Yang's belly and Zhi was six. Ling always said she was lucky to have lived in two countries, but Zhi always said that didn't count because Ling wasn't even born yet. Then Ling always said she wished her parents had left Zhi in China.

"See my robin!" Ellie waved her picture in the air. That would cheer her BFF up! This sketch had turned out especially well because she'd used her new lap desk. Her occupational therapist, Rachel, said it helped her sit up straighter when she drew outside. The smooth top was the perfect size for her nature notebook. Plus, it had a neck she could make as tall or as short as she wanted.

"I like the beak." Ling peeked over the rim of her sunglasses at Ellie's picture. "It's so pointy."

"Thanks, Ling!" Her BFF's words were as snuggly and warm as socks from the dryer. Especially after Ben had ignored her grasshopper drawing the night before.

Ling glanced over her shoulder. Then she said in a

whispery voice, "I have to tell you something."

"Me too!" Ellie had very important things to tell her best friend. Like how the robin she'd drawn was the newest member of the bird rock band. And how she hoped its round belly was full of chirpy babies.

"Let me go first, okay?" Ling pulled a familiar pink paper from her purse.

Ellie groaned as her BFF unfolded the marriage list. A list so top-secret that Ling usually kept it hidden in her unicorn diary. A list decorated with pink and purple nail polish and stickers that laid

Chapter 6

out the six steps to getting married

"Come on, El," Ling hissed. "This is important!"

But Ellie was sick of hearing her BFF talk about the marriage list. She wished Sophia, Ling's Best Ballet Friend, had never made it in the first place. Because now that was all Ling talked about. She said it helped her track how many steps were left until Zhi and Eddy got married and moved away. Then she could take over her sister's big bedroom with the walk-in closet.

"Let's hoop!" Ellie suggested, eager to distract her BFF. But Ling thrust the crumpled paper in front of her anyway.

"Zhi and Eddy are still stuck on the gross kissing step." Ling sighed and pointed at a sticker with smooching butterflies next to number four.

"Yuck!" Ellie shuddered, remembering her cousin, Jeff's, wedding last year. Luckily, Ben had been there to tell her when the kissing part had finally ended and it was safe to open her eyes.

Ling tapped a sticker of a glittery diamond ring by number five. "Why hasn't Eddy bought Zhi an engagement ring yet? *Why?*" she howled. "At this rate, I'll never get her walk-in closet! And that means I'll never have enough room to hang my recital tutus in rainbow order!"

"She'll get her egg men wing soon," Ellie assured Ling, like always.

"*Engagement ring*," Ling said.

"Remember I told you engagement rings are like your extra sparkle ring, but they're for getting married."

"I know!" Ellie stood up, eager to try her new lime green hoop. It was heavier than Ling's. Lots of her AC friends had heavy hoops because they didn't spin as fast as skinny hoops.

"The good news is that Eddy got a job at Burger Barn," Ling continued. "Sophia says that means he'll have enough money for an engagement ring soon.

Chapter 6

Then they can *finally* get married!" She ran her finger over a funny sticker of two sloths in fancy wedding clothes by step number six. The final step. The step where Zhi and Eddy have a wedding and move away.

Ellie thought weddings were boring. In fact, she thought they were even more boring than the marriage list. Luckily, Ben had had the great idea to play rock paper scissors during the never-ending talking parts at Jeff's wedding.

"Hoop with me!" Ellie tried again and again to twirl the hoop around her middle, but it plopped down in the grass each time.

"Keep your shoulders still," instructed Ling who was a pro hooper.

After a few more tips, Ellie got one whole round!

"Good job," said Ling. "Now come here so we can talk, okay?"

"No!" Ellie panted, trying again. "Come hoop!"

Ling shook her head. "I don't want to get my qipao sweaty."

Qipao. That was the name of her Chinese dress!

"Besides, I have more to tell you," Ling continued. "And I have to be sitting down to break news like this."

Ellie gulped. "Break knees?"

"Break *news,* not *knees,*" said Ling. "It means I have to tell you something important."

Ellie liked hearing important things as much as she liked saying them. "Spill the beans, Ling!" She picked up her hoop again.

Ling took a deep breath. Then she said, "Ben and Sara are getting married too."

And as soon as those words hit Ellie's ears, her hoop hit the ground like a brick.

Chapter 7

"No way, Joséééé!" Ellie shouted, before collapsing in the grass next to Ling.

No way, José was almost as fun to say as *Spill the beans.* She'd heard *No way, José* once on a funny TV show and hadn't stopped using it since. At first, it had only been for silly things like when Ben asked if she wanted carrots instead of cheesy chips. But Ellie realized those three words worked for terrible things too.

Like finding out your brother was getting married.

"This is why it took me so long to tell you," Ling moaned. "I knew you'd be devastated!"

Ellie and the Marriage List

Ellie crawled miserably toward the trunk of her tree and leaned her back against the bumpy bark. Devastated must mean *really, really, really not happy.* Because that was exactly how she felt!

"I'm sorry for being a terrible BFF." Ling sat next to Ellie with the marriage list. "I was so busy worrying about Zhi and Eddy that I didn't notice Ben and Sara are already on step two!"

Ellie shook her head. It couldn't be true! Brothers weren't allowed to get married! *Were they?* Besides, Ben thought Jeff's wedding was as boring as she did! He'd never want one of his own!

Ling thrust the marriage list in front of Ellie again. "It's true! Look at the first step! Sophia says that's the *Act cool* step, remember? And Ben and Sara were for sure acting cool yesterday, right?"

"I don't know!" Ellie's eyes flicked to the sticker of a prince sunbathing by the castle pool next to number one. The worst part was his tall, stuck-in-one-place helmet hair. And if you looked closely, you

Chapter 7

could see a princess floating in a crown-shaped innertube behind him.

Ling pointed at the prince's big, shiny muscles. "Sophia says during the first step, boys like to show off their biceps and use lots of hair gel."

"Why?" The word popped out as dry and crunchy as a potato chip. Ellie should have paid more attention all the other times Ling had told her this stuff.

"The prince wants the princess to think he looks cool. Just like Ben and Sara are trying to look cool for each other," said Ling. "Get it?"

But Ellie was busy getting excited about that *other* sticker next to number one – a tube of sparkly lipstick. "Ben doesn't wear makeup!" she informed

Ellie and the Marriage List

Ling.

"But Sara does!" Ling said. "I saw her lip gloss shining from all the way across the street yesterday! Sophia says when girls wear lip gloss or lipstick it means they're getting ready for the kissing step."

Ellie gulped because Sara's lip gloss *had* been extra shiny yesterday. But then she remembered something great. "Grandma wears lipstick!" Ellie's grandma liked making pies, not acting cool!

Ling nodded. "Yep, she's probably acting cool for your grandpa! Sophia says—"

"I don't care!" Ellie was sick of hearing about Sophia. *Sophia was a bridesmaid at two weddings! Sophia tried real coffee! Sophia has three earring holes in each ear! Sophia can say a bad word in Spanish!*

"But if it wasn't for Sophia, we wouldn't have the marriage list. And if we didn't have the marriage list, how would you save Ben from getting married and moving away forever?" Ling asked.

Chapter 7

"He... He... He won't do that!" Just the thought made Ellie want to cry. Besides, Ben liked living with her, didn't he?

"Look at the hang out step if you don't believe me!" Ling tapped number two on the marriage list. A pair of cartoon monkeys dangled by their tails, each holding one side of a heart that said, *Let's hang together.* "Remember how excited I was when Zhi and Eddy started hanging out?"

"Uh-huh," mumbled Ellie.

"I *know* what I saw yesterday on the way to Dance World," Ling said. "Sara was so excited to *hang out* with Ben, she had to invade *your* hike! The one *you'd* been waiting forever for!"

At the mention of the ruined hike, Ellie's head ached, and her tummy churned.

"I know they work at

Albert's together," said Ling. "But Sophia told me hanging out doesn't count if you're getting paid."

Then Ellie told Ling that Sara sometimes went to the park to watch Ben's games and that Ellie sometimes saw them talking under her tree.

"Oh, Ellie! How could I have missed the signs?" Ling cried. "Next to Sophia, I know more about the marriage list than anyone on earth, but I still let you down!"

Without speaking, Ellie fished her triangle pencil from the grass.

"Why aren't you talking?" Ling asked as Ellie flipped open her nature notebook to the robin picture. "Are you in shock?"

"I'm drawing!" It felt good to drag the tip of her pencil in short, hard lines as she made the beak sharper and sharper.

"Ignoring it will only make things worse!" Ling poked out her chin. "They went through two whole steps in one afternoon! At this rate, Ben will move

Chapter 7

out before Zhi!"

As Ling spoke, Ellie wondered if she might be right. Maybe Ben would marry Sara and leave forever.

"We have to watch for the third step, okay?" Ling pointed at the marriage list again. "That's all we can do until we come up with a plan to stop Ben and Sara's wedding."

Ellie's breath caught at the sight of the mermaid and merman sticker next to number three. Not only were they swimming in a sparkly blue ocean, but they were holding hands!

Ling touched Ellie's arm. "So, let me know right away if you see Ben and Sara holding hands, okay?"

Looking at that sticker,

Ellie and the Marriage List

Ellie was flooded with memories from yesterday's soggy sprint home. And it wasn't long before she'd told Ling what she'd seen.

"Are you sure?" Ling grabbed Ellie's shoulders. "Are you sure you saw Ben and Sara holding hands?"

Ellie gave a sniffly nod.

"This is worse than I thought!" Ling shook her head. "Ben and Sara are now officially on number three! One step behind Zhi and Eddy!"

Chapter 8

Ling paced the shady grass beneath the weeping willow. "It will be okay!" she promised Ellie, who was more dejected than ever. "We'll find a way to stop Ben and Sara's wedding!"

"Let's tell them no!" Ellie jumped up to follow her.

"You can't just *tell* people they aren't allowed to get married," Ling said.

"Why?" Ellie wanted to know.

"Teenagers don't listen to anybody after their hormones grow in!" Ling stopped to face Ellie. "Just look at Zhi! She's full of hormones! Mom says that's why she's been so bossy lately."

Ellie's own mom said hormones were the reason

Ben had to wear deodorant that smelled like air freshener from the doctor's office bathroom.

Ling smoothed her already smooth-as-glass hair. "Sara follows Ben because her hormones are telling her he's cute."

"Ben isn't cute!" Ellie huffed. Tara's kitten, Oscar, was cute. But Ben just looked like a brother! Besides, she didn't want to talk about hormones anymore. Each time Ellie heard the word, she imagined crispy-shelled zombie beetles blowing smelly green clouds into Ben's armpits.

For a while, the girls went back and forth, trying to figure out a way to stop the wedding.

"I have an idea," Ling said finally. "I wasn't going to say it, but it's the only way."

"Tell me!" begged Ellie.

"So last night, Zhi and Eddy were watching one of those ghost-hunting shows. Mom wouldn't let me watch, but I heard everything from the kitchen. They interviewed this expert named the Ghost Guru

Chapter 8

who lives in a real haunted house!"

Ellie frowned. She didn't understand how this could save Ben.

"Everyone knows ghosts love nighttime," Ling continued, "But the Ghost Guru says they can *only* appear at midnight—no other times!"

"So?" Ellie shrugged.

"*Soooooooooo*...we thought the ballerina ghost was hiding up there every day waiting for it to get dark so she can dance, right?" Ling exclaimed, pointing at the treehouse. Ellie nodded. "Well, she isn't!"

"Really?" Ellie whispered, letting Ling's words settle in.

"Yep! And here's the best part," said Ling. "If the Ghost Guru is right, that means we must have seen the ballerina ghost at midnight! Sophia hasn't even stayed up until midnight!"

But Ellie's thoughts had bounced back to the scariest sleepover in the world. Her skin prickled at the fuzzy memory of little kid Ling sneaking out of her sleeping bag and tiptoeing to Ellie's window to see how creepy the treehouse looked at night.

But little kid Ellie had stayed safely nestled in her cocoon of pillows and stuffed animals. Between that pointy witch hat roof and those splintery walls, the treehouse was creepy enough to look at during the day. And without thick summer leaves to hide behind, the weeping willow was as bare and knobby as a skeleton hand.

Then Ling had started screeching about a ballerina ghost dancing in the treehouse. Terrified, Ellie had scrambled over to help, losing her glasses in the process. She had tried really hard not to look. But even with blurry, no-glasses eyes, the white thing glowing in the treehouse window had been impossible to miss.

Ellie's spooky thoughts were interrupted by the bird rock band striking up a happy tune.

"Isn't this great news?" Ling asked as the chirpy song tweeted on behind the girls. "With the ballerina

Chapter 8

ghost only in the treehouse at midnight, we have lots of other times to scare Sara!"

Ellie's ears perked up. "Scare Sara?"

Ling nodded. "We'll freak her out so much, she'll never come back!"

Ellie liked the sound of that. There was one important question though. "How?" she asked.

"We'll hide in the treehouse and make spooky ghost voices while she and Ben are under the weeping willow!" Ling explained breathlessly. "You told me that ghosts freak Sara out, right?"

"Right!" Ellie cheered. Sara *was* scared of ghosts! She'd said so on the ruined hike!

"We'll do it after one of Ben's soccer games while they're hanging out under your tree, okay?" Ling asked.

"Yes! Yes! Yes!" Ellie squealed.

The more they talked, the more excited Ellie got. So excited, she couldn't wait one more second to put their plan into action.

"Not yet!" Ling shrieked when Ellie reached for the rope ladder.

This wasn't the same ladder Ben had used when he was a kid. Rachel had helped Ellie's parents pick this one out because it was easier to climb. Not only was it anchored at the top and bottom, but the fat ropes on either side were smooth and easy to hold. There was even grippy tape on the wide planks to make her tennis shoes stick better.

"We aren't done planning!" Ling cried as Ellie grabbed one side of the ladder with each hand.

"Yes, we are!" Ellie replied. The sooner they scared Sara away the better.

"Just because you climb stuff in therapy doesn't mean you can climb a rope ladder!" Ling protested. "You need to train first! You have to get strong so you can climb fast. Besides, teenagers are hard to scare so we have to practice super terrifying ghost voices!"

"*ROOAAARRRR!*" Ellie growled as she lifted one foot onto the bottom plank.

Chapter 8

"You sound like a goose, not a ghost!" Ling huffed.

Goose or not, Ellie wasn't going to let anything stop her. For as long as she could remember, her parents and therapists had tried to convince her to play in the treehouse. *Climbing is great exercise! Ben used to love playing there! Don't you want to try?* And Ellie had always given them the same answer. *No way, José!*

But today was different thanks to the Ghost Guru.

Ellie lifted her other foot out of the grass and onto the bottom plank.

"No!" Ling cried. "You can't do it yet!"

"Yes, I can!" But with her weight fully on the ladder, Ellie wasn't so sure. It was wobblier than she'd expected. And the more Ellie tried *not* to wiggle, the more she did, which made her feel like she was riding a wild elephant trunk.

"Stop!" Ling tugged on Ellie's T-shirt.

Ellie tried to twist away, but the rope ladder only

swung harder. "Let go, Ling!"

"*You* let go of the rope ladder, then *I'll* let go!" Ling shot back, tugging some more.

Ellie tried to climb away. But between the swingy ladder, her tired muscles, Ling pulling on her, and some leftover ballerina ghost fear, Ellie's *entire body* felt as trembly as a spaghetti noodle. Slowly, she slid one hand up the rope ladder for one last try. But at that exact moment, Ling grabbed her waist.

"Stop it!" Ellie yelled.

"No!" Ling grunted and pulled one enormous pull.

Chapter 8

The girls screeched as they struggled, a tangle of arms, legs, and rope ladder.

That's when Ellie lost her grip, sending both girls hurling backward onto the grass.

Chapter 9

The next day, Ellie and her parents went to the park to watch Ben's soccer game. Ling tagged along even though Ellie was still a little mad at her.

"Sorry about yesterday, El." Ling's sundress swished as the girls walked the wide, grassy space between the playground and the soccer field where Ben was leading warm-up drills for his team.

"Don't pull people!" Ellie winced, remembering the tumble from the rope ladder.

"You're right," admitted Ling. "But if it makes you feel better, my qipao has a giant grass stain now."

Ellie shrugged because, to her, grass stains were

Chapter 9

like nature's pretty, green paint

"Getting unscared of something after being scared of it for so long is harder than I thought," Ling continued as they walked. "It was like I forgot all the Ghost Guru stuff when I saw you on that ladder."

When Ellie still didn't say anything, Ling clapped her hands. "I know! You can wear my fancy starfish dress to the AC dance to make up for it! It's perfect for the beach theme!"

"Okay." Ellie brightened a little even though she didn't think dresses were nearly as exciting as Ling did.

"Do you still want to do the plan though?" asked Ling. "The plan to stop Ben and Sara's wedding?"

"Yes, yes, yes!" Ellie shoved her sweaty bangs off her forehead. She wasn't giving up. She'd never give up on her brother!

From the sidelines of the soccer field, Mom and Dad waved to the girls. Luckily, Sara was working at Albert's, so she wasn't there to spoil the evening.

Ellie and the Marriage List

"Since you still want to go through with it," Ling said, "I have to tell you something important."

"What?" Ellie asked as Ben's coach used his megaphone to announce that the game was beginning.

"There's a new part to the marriage list," Ling whispered. "If we don't stop Sara, Ben will turn into a Hawaii husband!"

"A *what?*" Ellie stopped to look at Ling.

"A Hawaii husband," Ling repeated. "Sophia read a grown-up book with people kissing on the cover. She said all the married people in the book live in Hawaii. Plus, her neighbor's uncle just had a wedding and moved there last week."

Hawaii. The familiar word rattled around Ellie's head. Then she remembered *Lilo and Stitch*, one of her favorite movies. "Stitch lives there!"

Ling shook her head. "Sophia says Hawaii is only for lovebirds now."

Before Ellie could ask if lovebirds lived in her

tree, Ling said, "Hey! I just thought of something! Didn't your cousin turn into a Hawaii husband too? The one with the beard and bushy eyebrows?"

"Jeff?" Ellie gasped, realizing she hadn't seen him since his boring wedding last year.

Ling nodded. "Your mom told mine he moved someplace far away that started with an H. It might have been a G, but I'm pretty sure it was an H!"

This was terrible! Ellie's long-lost cousin was probably flying around Hawaii with all the other lovebirds at this very moment!

Ling pulled the marriage list from the pocket of her sundress. "Sophia gave me a new sticker after ballet." She pointed at number six. The last step. The getting married step.

Surprised to see a long gray sticker under the wedding sloths' feet, Ellie asked Ling why they were skateboarding.

"It's an airplane, not a skateboard. Hawaii is so far

away you have to fly over the ocean to get there," said Ling. "Sophia didn't have any Hawaii stickers, so she took this one from her little brother."

"Let's watch Ben," said Ellie who'd had enough wedding talk for one day.

"But training is more important!" Ling protested. "Since Ben and Sara are on turbo speed, we've got to start now! We'll strength train for two weeks, then when you're a little stronger we'll work on ghost voices, okay?"

With a sigh, Ellie agreed, even though to her two weeks seemed like forever.

Ling's voice softened. "This is the best chance we have, so you've got to trust me, okay?"

"Okay." Ellie nodded. She trusted her BFF very much—even after she'd yanked her off the rope ladder. So she took one last look at her brother, huddled with his teammates on the soccer field. Then she followed Ling to the playground to begin her training.

Chapter 10

For the next two weeks, they trained hard. Ling set up hula hoop obstacle courses and taught Ellie to ballet jump from one to the next.

That part wasn't very fun, and half the time she ended up in the grassy space between the hoops.

But they did

Chapter 10

cool training stuff too. Like balancing on overturned garden buckets and lifting full-to-the-brim watering cans. Ellie even leapt over Mom's favorite zinnias without touching a petal and walked across a jump rope turned tight rope laid in the grass.

It was Saturday, their last day of training, and the afternoon before the AC dance. They were back at the park to watch Ben in a tiebreaking game against the best team in the city. Mom and Dad sat in lawn chairs next to Ellie and Ling who were stretched out on a blanket waiting for the game to begin.

"Where's Sara?" Ling opened a bag of pretzels and offered one to Ellie.

"She's covering for Ben at work so he can be in the tiebreaker," Mom answered as the players jogged onto the field.

While the parents cheered, Ling whispered to Ellie, "Don't forget. It's our last training day. We have to find something wobbly. Something as wobbly as the rope ladder."

Ellie and the Marriage List

Ellie groaned because she just wanted to watch Ben and think about how the AC dance was almost here.

"Any ideas?" Ling asked, looking around the park.

"The swings?" Ellie suggested half-heartedly. During last Saturday's game, they'd taken turns standing on a playground swing while the other girl wiggled it back and forth in rope ladder fashion.

"Not wobbly enough," Ling said, licking a crystal of pretzel salt from her thumb.

Ellie pointed toward the playground. "The bouncy bridge!"

Ling grinned. "You're brilliant!"

A few minutes later, the girls had climbed the stairs of the play structure. Slides, monkey bars, and a fireman pole jutted off in all directions. To Ellie, it looked like a giant, mixed-up playground robot.

When she was little, her physical therapist, Neema, had taken her to the park a lot. They had bounced on the bridge like pirates riding a stormy

Chapter 10

sea and carried big rocks up and down the play structure stairs.

"I just thought of something," said Ling as they approached the bouncy bridge connecting the two platforms of the play structure.

"What?" Ellie asked, eager to start jumping.

"I can't bounce. Kids below will see up my dress." Ling pointed to the tiny cracks between the wooden slats of the bridge.

"You have to!" Ellie just wanted to get the last day of training over with.

"It's okay," Ling said. "I have the strongest legs and best balance in my whole ballet class. But you should still do it, okay?"

That was fine with Ellie. She thought the bouncy bridge was fun. "Who can bounce me?"

"Try by yourself first," Ling said. "Then we'll find some wild kids to bounce you."

Ellie grabbed the rope railing and stepped onto the saggy, creaky bridge. It didn't shake quite as much as the rope ladder. But it was close.

"Jump holding on first, okay?" Ling said. "Then with no hands."

Ellie tried, but it had been so long since she'd been on the bridge with Neema. She was bigger now, and the swaying bridge made her feet feel like bowling balls.

"Come on!" Ling called. "You can do it!"

Then Ellie did do it! She jumped four whole times holding the railing and three without!

And it turned out they didn't need to search for wild, bouncy kids because they showed up on their own. Two younger boys bounded onto the bridge. They landed on either side of Ellie, sending her feet flying.

"Hey!" She tried to keep her balance as they bounced harder and harder.

"What's wrong with you?" The shorter kid with an up-to-the-nose juice mustache laughed at Ellie. "Don't you know how to jump?"

Chapter 10

"Of course she does!" shouted Ling. "You guys are bouncing too hard to give her a chance!"

"Duh!" shouted the taller boy who had spiky hair. "It's a bouncy bridge!"

The first boy leapt in front of Ellie. "Get!" *Jump.* "Off!" *Jump.* "The!" *Jump.* "Bridge!"

"Don't tell my Best Friend Forever what to do!" Ling growled as the boys slammed up and down.

What nobody understood was that Ellie *wanted* to get off the bridge! But the kids just bounced harder, yelling, "*Three little zombies jumping on the bed!*"

Only Ellie wasn't a zombie—and she wasn't jumping! In fact, she was barely standing! Ellie tried to hold on, but the harder she tried, the more the scratchy rope railing bit into her palms. Just as she lost her grip, her glasses shot off her face.

"Stop jumping!" Ling cried. "She can't see!"

Ellie stumbled. Then her knees folded beneath her. Without her glasses, the colors of the park blurred and swirled like watercolors.

Suddenly, a pink streak flew onto the bridge. "I'll save you, Ellie!" Ling called.

It was her BFF in her watermelon-colored dress!

Ling handed Ellie her glasses as the wild jumping finally ended.

"Where are your moms?" Ling glared at the boys. "I'm telling on you guys!"

"Come on!" juice mustache kid said to spiky hair kid. "Let's get out of here!"

Quick as lightning, they took off across the platform and squeaked down the fireman pole.

Chapter 10

"I'm going after them!" Ling yelled.

"Stay here!" Ellie begged because she wanted to forget all about those boys.

As the girls walked back across the platform, Ling pulled Ellie into the tiny covered alcove above the twisty slide.

"I don't... I don't..." Ellie's mouth muscles were tired. Her whole body was worn out.

"You don't what?" Ling whispered.

Ellie hugged her knees to her chest in the small space and she told Ling she didn't want to slide.

"Me neither. Sliding is babyish." Ling leaned in so close their noses touched.

But Ellie didn't want to slide because those boys had left a prickly, not-happy feeling in her chest. And because *Three little zombies jumping on the bed!* wouldn't stop echoing in her head.

"But we need privacy," Ling said, reaching into the pocket of her watermelon dress. "Nobody can see me give you the marriage list in here."

Ellie and the Marriage List

Ellie must have heard Ling wrong. "What?" she croaked.

"The marriage list," Ling repeated. "Sophia gave it to me when I needed it most. Now I'm doing the same for you."

Ellie swatted at the wrinkly pink paper in her BFF's hand. "You keep it!"

But Ling said she had the marriage list memorized. "Besides, Eddy and Zhi only have two steps left. You've got to keep track of Sara and Ben by yourself in case I'm at ballet or something. Otherwise, they could fly through the steps and move to Hawaii before we can stop them!"

As Ling pressed the square of paper into her palm, Ellie peeked out the tiny alcove window just in time to see Ben zooming toward the goal with the ball. Players from the other team raced behind, trying to catch him.

Ellie sighed because she knew exactly how they felt.

Chapter 11

"Hey, guess what?" Ben said the next day. Mom and Dad were upstairs getting ready for the dance while the kids finished an afternoon snack.

"What?" Ellie, who was a big fan of *guess whats*, looked up from her peanut butter toast.

Ben had on that same goofy grin she'd seen so much lately. "There will be *two* DJs at the AC dance this year."

"Two?" Ellie set down her cup of apple juice.

"Yep!" Ben nodded. "Sara is going to DJ too!"

Suddenly the peanut butter toast and juice felt as bubbly as lava in Ellie's throat.

"She surprised me last night," Ben continued

excitedly. "Albert even gave her the day off so she could help at the dance. Luckily, he understands because—"

Ben's phone rang. "Hey, Sara!" he answered.

Ellie's eyes prickled with tears. Not only would her BFF have to miss the AC dance for the first time ever, but now Sara would be there to ruin it! Just like the hike!

"Yep," Ben said into the phone as he winked at Ellie. "I just told her! She's so excited, I think she's in shock!"

Ellie couldn't take it anymore. She burst out of her chair, grabbed her nature notebook and triangle pencil from the counter, then took off out the back door. Halfway across the yard, she realized she didn't have her lap desk. But she wasn't going back. Not after what Ben said.

A few moments later, Ellie slumped against the trunk of her tree. For the first time ever, her fingers were too upset to draw. *What would she do now? How could she chase away her grumpy feelings if she couldn't even pick up her pencil?*

"Come on, Ellie!" Mom called from the back door. "Ling's here to help you get ready for the dance!"

When Ellie didn't move, Ling raced across the backyard. "Let's go! I laid my starfish dress on your bed!"

Ellie didn't even look up.

"If you want me to curl your hair, you better hurry because I've got to get ready for Zhi's boring concert soon."

Ling helped Ellie get ready for the AC dance every year. It was the only day Ellie liked being fancy, but she liked being fancy *with* Ling.

"Oh! Speaking of the most annoying sister in the universe." Ling smiled a giant smile. "Sophia said Eddy will probably propose to Zhi on stage tonight after her violin solo! She says lots of people give engagement rings that way, so everyone will cheer for them!"

Ellie smooshed her eyes shut. *There will be two DJs at the AC dance this year!* The words played over and over in her head.

"Oh! I thought of another cool thing! Maybe Zhi will forget to pack her beauty stuff when she moves out! Then we can have a spa day, okay? We'll do face masks and—" Ling stopped talking and sighed. "I know you're not sleeping, Ellie Anderson, so stop faking!"

One at a time, Ellie peeled her eyes open and looked at her best friend.

"Why are you being like this?" Ling demanded. "I just told you Eddy and Zhi are about to get engaged *and* it's the day of the AC dance!"

"I'm not going!" Ellie sputtered.

"What?" Ling shrieked. "Why—"

"Hurry up, El!" Ben called from the back door, interrupting Ling. "Sara's on her way. She's coming early with us to set up the DJ booth!"

Ling gasped. "Did he say what I think he said?"

Ellie nodded.

"Now I understand why you don't want to go!" Ling looked horrified after Ellie told her what her brother had said in the kitchen. "I bet Sara and Ben will get to the kissing step tonight! Lots of people kiss at dances."

Ellie tried to tell Ling she didn't want to hear any more. But her words ran together like alphabet soup. She yanked the marriage list from her pocket and glared at those kissing butterflies next to step four.

"What are you doing?" Ling asked as Ellie shoved the list back in her pocket and stood up.

But she didn't know what she was doing or where

she was going as she began running. She just wanted to feel better.

Only she didn't get far before she ran smack dab into the rope ladder.

And that gave Ellie an idea.

A great idea.

Chapter 12

Ellie grabbed the rope ladder with both hands. It was the first time she'd touched it since ending up in the grass two weeks before.

"Ellie!" Ling rushed over. "Wait!"

Ellie didn't answer. She was too busy staring up into the black hole that led into the treehouse. From here it looked like a monster mouth ready to gobble her up. But little kid Ben hadn't been scared. He'd crawled through that same hole lots of times.

Now it was Ellie's turn to be brave.

She set one foot on the bottom plank, then the other.

"What are you doing?" Ling shrieked.

"Hiding!" Ellie growled. With her weight fully on the ladder, it swung a little. But not too much. This was much easier than last time!

"Ellie, don't you see?" Ling cried. "There's no point in hiding from Sara when she's at the dance!"

"I'm hiding...from...EVERYONE!" Ellie panted. She swung her leg up onto the next plank a little too hard, making the ladder wave back and forth. But Ellie held on tight. She wasn't letting go. Not this time.

"We aren't good at ghost voices yet!" Ling grabbed the ladder to steady it.

"Stay back!" Ellie warned, inching higher. Ellie didn't like using such a grumpy voice with her BFF. But she didn't know what else to do with the tornado of feelings whipping around inside.

"I won't pull you!" Ling promised. "Just come down, okay?"

"No way, José!" Ellie shot back. She climbed in a shaky sort of rhythm. *Hand, foot, hand, foot...*

Chapter 12

"If they find you, our plan is ruined!" Ling's voice trembled. "Everyone will know you're not scared of the treehouse anymore!"

For once, Ellie wished Ling would stop talking.

But she didn't stop. "If you're in the treehouse, you won't know if Ben and Sara sneak a kiss at the dance!"

Just when Ellie couldn't take it anymore, she spotted something amazing. Something that made her forget her terrible morning. From a nearby branch, Banana, her favorite squirrel, wagged his crooked tail at her. Just like Banana was Ellie's favorite squirrel, Ellie was Banana's favorite person because she'd rescued him after he'd gotten trapped in their trashcan last

summer. Ever since then, Ellie's tree had been his playground and his home.

"I brought my starfish barrettes," Ling called from below. "They match the dress perfectly and—"

"I'M...NOT...GOING!" Ellie focused on Banana. Only Banana. He chattered and squeaked, like he was cheering her on. If she could save his life, she could climb into the treehouse!

Ling made one final attempt. "What if the Ghost Guru is wrong? What if the ballerina ghost *does* hide up there during the day?"

But nothing could make Ellie turn back now. That gaping hole was so close that the cool, shivery breath of the treehouse leaked onto her face. Then, as she climbed the last two planks, Ling said something wonderful.

"Wow, Ellie! You made it! You really are getting stronger!"

Between Banana rooting for her and Ling's words bouncing around her head, Ellie *did* feel stronger.

Chapter 12

Stronger than ever! Her tree-climbing muscles really had grown extra big from all the training. But her I-will-not-go-to-the-dance feelings had grown extra big too. Together, they made her as powerful as a gorilla!

Ellie squeezed her eyes shut and poked her head into the treehouse. It smelled as old and rotten as the bologna sandwich she'd accidentally left in her

lunchbox over Christmas break.

"If you see her pointe shoes, don't touch them, okay?" Ling called. "They're probably cursed!"

Slowly, slowly, Ellie opened one eye. Then the other. Daylight squeezed through the dirty window, casting a dusty beam of light across the small space.

"Ellie?" Ling called. "What's up there?"

"It's empty!" Her voice cracked as she took in the splintery walls, dead leaves scattered on the floor, and rickety door leading to the slide. All of it made her want to curl up in the warm grass below where everything was bright, green, and alive.

Then, from somewhere across the yard, Ben called, "Hey, Ling!"

Ellie gasped. She had to get into the treehouse, and she had to do it now! Just in time, she grabbed the skinny rungs Dad had nailed to the treehouse floor and scrambled inside.

"Where's Ellie?" Ben asked Ling. His voice was closer now. Much closer.

Chapter 12

"In the bathroom," Ling replied.

"But her nature notebook is right here!" Ben said.

"It was an emergency," Ling replied shakily. "She put me in charge of it until she comes back."

"She better hurry," said Ben. "Otherwise we won't have time to set up at the AC."

Ellie huddled against the cardboard-thin treehouse wall listening to their voices drift through the monster mouth hole. She tried not to think about the ballerina ghost dancing on this very floor. She tried not to think about the marriage list. She especially tried not to think about what a bad girl she was for hiding from her family.

Instead, she focused on her extra sparkle ring. Even in the murky gloom of the treehouse, it seemed to glitter and spark like a tiny green flame.

Chapter 13

"Hey, Ling! Can you take a picture of Ben and me?"

Ellie winced when Sara's voice joined the others. She crawled to the window which was open just enough to catch a breeze of backyard air. Ellie peeked out, but it was hard to see between the tangled leaves and branches.

"It's too hot out here. Let's go inside for pictures." Ling sounded quivery, like she'd just downed a jar of spicy salsa.

"But I want the tree in the background," said Sara. "Don't you, Ben?"

"I'm cool with whatever you want." Of course Ben didn't grumble like he did when Mom took his

Chapter 13

picture.

A moment later, all three wandered into Ellie's view directly beneath the treehouse. Blue surfboards covered Ben's button-up shirt, and his hair was crunchier and more stuck-in-one-place than ever.

Sara wore a white seashell-patterned dress and the yellow curls in her hair looked like swirls of cupcake frosting. And there was a bag from Albert's in her hand—the same kind Ben brought Ellie cheesy chips in.

"Hey, kids," Dad called from across the yard. "Where's the belle of the ball?"

"She's in the bathroom!" Ben yelled as Sara showed Ling how to work the camera on her phone.

After Dad took off to check the bathrooms, Ling backed up to get a full body shot.

"I love your Hawaiian shirt, Ben!" Sara crooned.

Hawaiian shirt? Had it come from Hawaii? This was a bad sign! A very bad sign!

"The DJ has to stand out!" Ben said.

"But I see you figured out that part of the job."

"What do you mean?" Sara's voice dripped sweet as honey.

"I mean you look...really...pretty."

Pretty? Ellie frowned. Ben said stuff like *Epic! Sweet! Cool!* But not *pretty!*

Sara giggled and fluffed her cupcake hair. "Oh, thank—"

"Say cheese!" Ling shouted.

Ben and Sara squished together.

"CHEEEESSEEEE!" they sang.

Stinky, yucky, getting-married cheese!

"Hey, Ling, can you see what's taking Ellie so long?" Ben asked. "I have to load the speakers into the car."

Don't go, Ling!

But Ling did go.

Now it was just Ellie, Ben, and Sara!

Ellie had never expected to do the scare-Sara-away-for-good plan today. And she'd never expected

Chapter 13

to do it without her BFF. Especially when her ghost voice still sounded like a honky goose.

But there they were. Ben and Sara were alone under her tree. And Ellie was ready. She was ready to do the biggest thing she'd ever done. Her body felt extra alive—like a baby bird busting out of her shell to face the world.

"Before you pack the car," Sara said to Ben. "Can I tell you something?"

"Sure," Ben replied. "What's up?"

"I already said this part, but I love my cookies." Sara held up the Albert's bag.

Ben bought Sara cookies? Ellie yanked the marriage list out of her pocket. Luckily, she didn't find a cookie sticker, but somehow the cheesy chips Ben brought her didn't seem so special now.

"The cookies are just a thank you," said Ben. "It's super cool you gave up your day to help at Ellie's dance."

"I want to help." Sara took a step closer to Ben.

"You don't have to thank me."

"Of course I do." Ben shrugged. "Besides, chocolate chip is your favorite."

"Nobody's ever given me cookies," Sara said. "Well, except my grandma at Christmas. But that doesn't count."

"Don't tell her that!" Ben laughed. "And homemade totally trumps cookies from Albert's!"

"I just mean, umm." Sara fiddled with the handles of the bag. "A boy. A boy has never given me cookies before."

"Really?" Ben asked. "I guess that's good news for me."

If only Ling were there. She'd know what all of this meant!

"There's another thing too, Ben," Sara said so quietly Ellie barely heard her. "But I'm nervous to tell you."

Ellie's knees burned from the grubby floor. She tried to shift her weight, but

Chapter 13

something poked at her hip through her shorts. *What was that?* She reached into her pocket—the pocket without the marriage list— and pulled out the tube of fox-colored paint. She'd been carrying it around since the day of the hike because it made her feel like a grown-up artist. Plus, she wanted to be ready if a fox ventured into her backyard.

"Why are you nervous?" Ben asked Sara. "Is it something bad?"

"*I* don't think it's bad. I mean, I think it's great." Sara shook her head. "I guess I sound like a real dork now."

"You're the coolest dork I know." Ben's words seemed like teasing words. But his voice wasn't the teasing one Ellie knew.

"What I want to say is," Sara looked up at Ben. "You can kiss me, if you want to."

Then she puckered up her lips like two shiny worms.

Ellie and the Marriage List

Ellie tried not to scream as she fumbled for the marriage list again. Those awful kissing butterflies reminded her she was almost a step closer to losing Ben.

And outside, things were just getting worse. Ben and Sara's faces zoomed closer and closer. With a grunt, Ellie shoved the window all the way up and poked her head out. So what if her ghost voice sounded a little goosey? She had to do something to stop them!

Just as her brother's mouth came in for a landing, Ellie let out a howl. "*Wooooooooooooo!*"

"Whoa!" Ben pulled away from Sara just in time. "What was that?"

"It sounded like a sick owl or something!" Sara cried, looking up.

Ellie ducked into the treehouse before she could be spotted. But then everything was quiet. Very

Chapter 13

quiet. Ellie peeked outside again and groaned. Sara and Ben were back in kissing position!

No way, José! No way, José! No way, José! Ellie bit her lip to keep the words from spilling out. Her ghost voice hadn't worked!

And now they were practically kissing!

Ellie barely felt her fingers unscrew the cap on the fox-colored paint. This time, she jammed the whole top of her body out the window. Ellie had to stop this kiss! And she had to do it now!

But she wasn't fast enough.

As their lips touched, Ellie aimed the tube of orange paint right over Sara's head.

Then, with shaking fingers, she squeezed.

She squeezed with every rope-ladder climbing muscle she had.

Chapter 14

"Ahhhh!" Sara screamed. "That owl pooped on me!"

Ben circled the tree, peering up into the branches. "You were right about it being sick if it has poop that color!"

Ellie tried to wriggle back inside, but she was stuck in the tiny window frame!

Below, Sara frantically wiped at the paint, smearing it across the front of her dress like pumpkin guts. "Maybe Ellie is right! Maybe that treehouse really is haunted!"

Finally! The words Ellie had been waiting for! It was working! Her goosey, sick owl ghost voice was working! She tried again. "*Booooooooooooo!*" By now her tongue was as dry and floppy as a woolen sock so she sounded extra scary!

But instead of running away, Sara pointed right at her. "Hey! Look up there!"

Now Ben was staring at her too. "Ellie? What are you doing in the treehouse?"

Like a bee trapped in honey, Ellie struggled to free herself.

Ben came closer, his eyes zoning in on her.

"Everyone is looking for you!" His voice was as sharp as the tip of her triangle pencil. "What are you doing up there?"

How could she answer such a question? How would she ever explain when she felt so mixed up inside? If only she could turn into Banana. She'd scamper all the way up to the tip top of her tree and snuggle up by the bird rock band stage. A place with no lip gloss, crunchy hair, or sloths in wedding dresses. A place with no busy brothers or endless soccer practices.

Chapter 14

A peaceful place.

Finally, with one giant twisty yank, Ellie shot backward onto the floor, the window slamming shut behind her.

That's when more voices leaked through the monster mouth hole.

Mom and Dad: *Where's Ellie? We've been tearing the house apart looking for her!*

Ben: *She's in the treehouse! I just saw her.*

Mom: *Your sister? In the treehouse? Please be serious, Ben!*

Dad: *Your mom is right, son. We all know your sister has herself all worked up over that mermaid ghost. She'd never set foot in the treehouse!*

Ling: *Ballerina ghost, Mr. Anderson. Whoa, Sara! Your hair! I hope you have a good clarifying shampoo!*

Mom: *Oh dear, Sara, what happened to you?*

Ben: *That's a question for Ellie. Come on, El! Come down the slide and I'll catch you.*

But Ellie was already crawling towards the door

that led to the yellow-as-a-lemon slide.

"This is no time for jokes, Ben!" Dad boomed. "Your sister isn't in that treehouse!"

Ellie pushed the treehouse door open. "Yes, I am."

"See!" Ben said, "I told you guys!"

"Oh, sweetie! We've been searching high and low!" Mom rushed over, tripping on the hem of her sailboat-print skirt.

Dad, who was wearing his magician suit, caught Mom before she faceplanted in the grass. But his eyes were on Ellie.

Everyone's eyes were on Ellie.

She'd done a terrible thing! Nobody would like her now. Not even her own family!

"You had us very worried, Ellie," Dad said. Then he paused like he was thinking about something. "And how on earth did you get up there by yourself?"

Ellie stared at her legs stretched out on the slide, ready for takeoff.

Chapter 14

"Come on, El," Ben prompted. "Answer Dad."

"I bet the custom ladder I installed had something to do with it!" Dad puffed out his chest. "Is that right, sweetie?"

Ellie nodded, but she couldn't find the right words to say.

"That's my strong girl!" Dad fist pumped the air. "I knew you'd overcome your fear of the princess ghost!"

"Ballerina ghost!" Ling squeaked.

"This really is a wonderful accomplishment," said Mom. "But let's be certain one of your therapists is here for your next climb so you can learn the safest way."

Next climb? No way, José!

Then Ben stepped forward. "El," he said. "How did Sara get that orange stuff all over her?"

"Umm... I..." Ellie stammered, realizing that the deflated tube of grown-up paint was still tucked in her sweaty palm.

"Ellie." Dad straightened his bow tie. "Did you have something to do with what happened to Sara?"

"No!" Ling shouted. "Ellie doesn't do stuff like that!"

But Ellie opened her fingers and let the wrinkled, used-up tube drop to the grass. "Yes, I do!"

Ling gasped and scooped it up. "I didn't know you took paint up there!"

"You knew Ellie was in the treehouse?" Ben glared at Ling. "Why did you tell us she was in the bathroom?"

Mom sighed. "You should have let us know, Ling."

"Ling...said...not to!" Ellie pushed the heavy, sticky words out of her mouth. She couldn't bear for Ling to take the blame after she'd begged Ellie to stay out of the treehouse.

Chapter 14

"Come down so we can talk about this!" said Mom in her I-mean-business voice.

"Then you can give Sara a proper apology," said Dad.

As angry as Ellie was at Sara for turning Ben into a Hawaii husband, the sight of her standing behind the others with her orange-streaked hair and droopy, spotted dress made Ellie wish she hadn't done such a terrible thing.

But she was glad when Ben got into position at the end of the slide. At least he still loved his sister enough to catch her!

Finally, Ellie pushed off and sailed down the slide into Ben's arms. At the same time, a fox-colored tear slipped down Sara's cheek.

Then, before anyone could stop her, Sara took off out of the yard without looking back.

Chapter 15

The car ride to the AC dance wasn't like last year. Or any of the years before.

Ellie's family was quiet. Very quiet.

There was no music blasting from the stereo or car dancing. There was no betting who could eat the most mini cupcakes.

They were going to be late all because of her. Ellie had heard Mom say so on the phone to the other AC parents. "I'm sorry. Ellie had an...incident...at home, but we're on our way now."

Ben sat by Ellie in the back, checking his phone because Sara wasn't responding to his texts. This *should* be good news. After all, Ellie wanted Sara to

Chapter 15

leave Ben alone. But it was hard to be happy when her brother was so *unhappy*.

Ellie slumped in her seat and glared at the pink egg pattern on her itchy, too-small Easter dress. That was the other terrible thing. Mom had said she didn't deserve to wear Ling's starfish dress after what she'd done.

"Did you act out because you wanted Ling to come to the dance? Is that it?" Mom turned to look at her from the passenger seat.

Without looking up, Ellie shook her head.

"As we told you," Dad said. "We're proud that you accomplished such a feat. But why go in the treehouse today of all days?"

"Good question," muttered Ben.

Spiky caterpillar hair, kissy lip gloss lips, Hawaii husbands and lovebirds! I miss Ben! Ben does not miss me! Putting the words together like puzzle pieces seemed impossible.

"Sometimes when we're confused or upset,

feelings come out in ways we don't expect," Dad said. "I went through a period when I was so dejected in my magician job search that I tried my hand at baking."

The whole car groaned at the memory of rock-hard biscuits and burnt-to-a-crisp cookies.

"Hey, now!" Dad said. "I had to put that energy somewhere. But the important thing is to find the right place to release it!"

"Baking was not the right choice for your father, and squirting paint on Sara—or anyone for that matter—certainly wasn't the right choice for you, Ellie," said Mom.

Ellie turned her extra sparkle ring on her finger. "I know."

"We shouldn't have left the rope ladder up." Dad stopped at a red light. "Your mother and I take some blame in this too."

"We thought it would be years before you outgrew your ballerina ghost fear," Mom sighed. "But you

Chapter 15

have certainly taught us to never say never."

"It's cool you got over the whole haunted treehouse thing, El," Ben said a moment later. "But why would you do that? Why would you squeeze paint on Sara?"

"Because!" Ellie stared out the window at cars and trucks whizzing by.

"Because why?" Mom, Dad, and Ben asked at the same time.

Ellie kept her lips closed tight. If she opened them, stuff about the marriage list might spill out. Then Ling would be mad at her too. And Ellie would know more mad people than not-mad people.

The car got quiet again. So quiet, Ellie couldn't stand it. "I'm sorry!" she blurted. But those words seemed so tiny. Like two itty-bitty drops at the bottom of an empty pool.

"We're glad," said Dad as they pulled into the AC parking lot. "But Sara is the one who really needs an apology."

"We'll have a family meeting about it tomorrow," said Mom as they got out of the car.

Her parents were right, but Ellie felt worse than ever. Maybe it was because family meetings were always bad news. During the last one, they'd found out that Grandma needed a knee operation. In the one before that, Ellie had gotten stuck with playroom dusting duty. *Yuck!* Her too-pink, too-boring basement playroom. Mom had decorated it while Ellie was still in her tummy. That was before she knew Ellie didn't like bubble-gum-colored *indoor* playrooms. And before she realized Ellie liked leafy-green *outdoor* stuff.

But maybe Ellie felt worse because Ben didn't ask her to help unload the DJ equipment. Usually, she got to carry something important, like his microphone or the cord for his speaker, but this year it was like her brother forgot she was even there.

Chapter 16

When Ellie walked through the Ability Center doors, she had prickly about-to-cry eyes. Not only were Ben and Sara officially on the kissing step, but her too-small Easter dress was itchier than a full-body mosquito bite, her scraped-up knees stung from the splintery treehouse floor, and her bottom hurt from launching backward out of the window.

But knowing that her family was disappointed in her was worse than all those feelings squished together.

Tara, who wore an octopus costume and paper seaweed necklace, was the first to greet her. She wrapped Ellie in a hug and patted her hair. Even though her favorite AC friend couldn't talk much, Tara understood lots of things. Like how Ellie was feeling.

Maria, their speech therapist, said Tara was a good communicator. That meant she didn't need a lot of words to tell people how she felt. Tara cried when she was sad—like the time her kitten, Oscar, got stuck behind the washing machine. And when she was happy, she jumped, giggled, gave high fives and shouted "Yay!" Tara was like most kids, but without so many words mixed in.

Ellie held one of Tara's eight arms as they made

Chapter 16

their way around the AC gym. Sea-blue spotlights bounced like ping pong balls off the walls and floor. Cardboard sharks dangled from the ceiling, and the sound of their friends having fun tickled Ellie's ears.

The girls stopped to say hi to Maria who wore a *Speech at the Beach* T-shirt. She was helping kids spell their favorite ocean animal names in trays of sand with their fingers. Then they waved to Neema who was leading some other kids in a warmup for the hokey pokey, the first song of every AC dance.

Across the room, Rachel led a group of kids in a swimming-without-water class. She wore a puffy gray costume and a big smile. "Doggie paddle for ten seconds! Faster! Faster! There's a crocodile after us! Follow *meeeeee*, the OT *manateeeeeee!*" The kids shrieked and giggled, scooping at the air.

"Where's your beach clothes?" asked a boy named Marc wearing a crab costume. Marc was the kind of kid who always asked the wrong questions at the wrong time.

Ellie tugged on her too-small-mosquito-bite-Easter dress, wishing more than ever that it was Ling's starfish one with the matching barrettes.

Her friend Kendra pointed at her and said, "Fish eggs!"

Ellie looked down. The pattern on her dress *did* look like fish eggs! "Yes, fish eggs!" Ellie smiled gratefully at Kendra who wore a pirate costume complete with an eye patch and a toy parrot for her shoulder. Even her hot pink wheelchair was decorated like a pirate ship with a poster board sail.

Marc shrugged and took off to join some kids chanting, "Music! Music! Music!" around the DJ booth while Dad and Ben hurried to set up.

That gave Ellie an idea. Ben probably needed her to be the volume helper like last year! She'd sat next to the speaker while he'd pointed up for louder and down for quieter.

Ellie told Tara her plan on their way to the DJ booth. Once Ben remembered what a great volume

Chapter 16

helper she was, he'd remember what a great sister she was too!

But Marc was standing in front of the speaker with his crab claw blocking the volume knob.

"Excuse me," Ellie said, just like Mom had taught her.

Marc didn't move. "I'm DJ Ben's helper!" he announced.

"No, I am!" Ellie shot back. She looked at Ben who was slipping his headphones on.

"He asked first, okay, El?" Ben said. "You did it last year."

Ellie couldn't believe it. How could Ben choose Marc over her? Marc would press all the wrong buttons just to see what happened! Ellie, on the other hand, was a very careful volume helper! She knew exactly what to do!

"Please, Ben?" Ellie called as Tara squeezed her hand. But with his headphones on, he couldn't hear her.

"Hey, AC crew!" Ben's voice boomed over the microphone. "Let's get this party started!"

The crowd cheered as the familiar music roared to life. Everyone formed a wiggly, giggly circle on the dance floor.

Everyone except Marc who was sitting on the speaker like it was his throne.

Chapter 17

You put your left foot in, you take your left foot out.
You put your left foot in and shake it all about!
Do the hokey pokey and you turn yourself around!
That's what it's all about!

Sure, lots of kids didn't know left or right. Some couldn't stand on one foot. But it didn't matter. Ellie liked how nobody told them they were wrong. Besides, Neema, Maria, and Rachel were there to help if anyone needed it. But mostly, kids just did what felt good.

With the music playing, a new energy grew inside of Ellie. It felt good to move her muscles and laugh with her friends. And she felt lighter without the marriage list there to weigh her down. It was at home under her pillow since her easter dress didn't have pockets.

During the *Put your whole body in and shake it all about* part, Kendra's mom spun her wheelchair in the center while everyone danced around them. Some kids jumped. Others did the robot. A couple of shy kids stood by their parents bobbing their heads to the beat. Tara bounced while Ellie did a little of everything, even a ballet jump in honor of Ling. She was having so much fun, she almost forgot about crabby Marc hogging her volume helper job.

By the time Mom announced that the snack table was open, Ellie was starving. While everyone munched on under-the-sea Jell-O, shark-shaped pretzels, seashell cookies and veggies with dip dyed ocean blue, Dad set up a table at the front of the gym for the magic show.

"Put your hands together for Martin the

Chapter 17

Magnificent!" Ben announced when it was time for the show to begin.

Ellie cheered louder than anyone as Dad waved to the audience. She thought he looked like a handsome penguin in his black and white magician suit.

He performed all of Ellie's favorites like the flying shoe trick and the floating flamingo trick. He even poured disappearing ink on Tara's octopus arm and pulled a banana out of Ben's ear.

"I'd like to invite my daughter, Ellie, up to help me with the grand finale!" Dad announced, aiming his wand at her.

With everything going on, Ellie had almost forgotten that Dad had promised she could help with the grand finale trick! He must not be too mad if he was letting her do something so important.

First, he let Ellie put the coconut in his hat. Then, he took her hand and held it up for the crowd to see. "Behold! Something more powerful and more mystical than any magician's wand!"

The crowd whispered, wondering what Martin the Magnificent was talking about.

Ellie didn't know either. Did Dad think she'd sprouted magic fingernails? But he pointed at Ellie's ring. "My daughter's extra sparkle! The brightest, most magical light in my life!" The crowd hooted and clapped like she was a movie star.

Then Ellie waved her hand over Dad's hat, imagining glittery stars shooting from her fingertips.

Except for a kid named Brent with a burping problem, the

Chapter 17

gym was silent.

"Abracadabra!" Ellie shouted
at the top of her lungs. Even the R
sounds came out almost perfect!

On the sidelines, Maria cried, "Go, Ellie!"
because they'd been working on that word a lot
since Dad had said she could help with the coconut
trick.

Together, Ellie and Dad flipped over the magician
hat. It worked! The coconut was nowhere to be seen.

Dad and Ellie took a bow, and the crowd went
wild again. Then, as Ben played the closing song,
Tara slipped her paper-seaweed necklace around
Ellie's neck.

"That was quite a performance you two put on!"
A tall man with a booming voice approached.

"Thanks!" said Ellie, admiring her new necklace.

"We're glad you enjoyed it!" Dad said as he packed
up his props.

"I certainly did," replied the man. "Where are

my manners? My name is Ted Larkin. I'm Brent's uncle."

Dad shook his hand. "I'm Martin the Magn—I mean, I'm Martin Anderson, and this is my daughter, Ellie."

Once the introductions were complete, Mr. Larkin said, "I just spoke to your wife." He motioned to the back of the gym where Mom was helping the other parents clean up. "She mentioned you're looking for a magician job."

The plastic flamingo in Dad's hand clattered to the floor as he looked up at Mr. Larkin. "As a matter of fact, I am!"

"Well, it just so happens I've been searching high and low for a reliable magician to join my company," Mr. Larkin said.

As the AC dance came to an end, Ellie watched a grin so big and magnificent stretch across Dad's face, she forgot all about those about-to-cry feelings she'd walked in the door with.

Chapter 18

"I'll know more about the magician position after my lunch meeting with Ted today," Dad said at breakfast the next morning. "But first things first." His eyes landed on Ellie.

"Your father's right," said Mom. "Family meeting time, everyone."

Ellie gazed out the window, wishing she was under the weeping willow. Anywhere but here.

"I'm taking down that rope ladder until your therapists can give you some safety tips," said Dad as he refilled his coffee mug.

"Don't worry, sweetie," Mom said to Ellie. "They'll have you climbing again in no time."

"Then you can play in the treehouse whenever you want," added Dad.

"No way, José!" Ellie muttered as she stirred a cereal tornado in her bowl. She didn't want to set foot on that rope ladder ever again.

"What's wrong, sweetie?" Mom asked. "You don't want to play in the treehouse?"

"No way, José!" Ellie growled again.

"Even José would say you're wearing out his name, El." Ben gulped down the last of his orange juice.

Ellie tried to explain. The treehouse was creepy, stinky, and dirty! Besides, her poor weeping willow wanted to be a stage for the bird rock band and a playground for Banana and his friends. It didn't want to hold a haunted treehouse!

Ben checked his watch. "I have to be at the field in twenty minutes." He stood up. "I'll check on Sara on my way."

Ellie stirred harder making her spoon clang against the bowl. *No! No! No!* Even though Sara

Chapter 18

hadn't run off in the way Ellie and Ling had planned, at least she was gone. The last thing Ellie wanted was for Ben to lure her back in!

"This won't take long, son," Dad said. "Besides, Sara is a big part of this meeting."

Ellie made such a big cereal tornado that bits of soggy Fruit Loops flew through the air like confetti.

"You're making a mess, honey." Mom handed her a dish towel.

As Ellie mopped up, Dad said, "The choices you made yesterday impacted a lot of people."

"Especially Sara," said Ben.

"Especially Sara," echoed Mom and Dad.

"But why is she ignoring *me*?" Ben frowned. "What did *I* do wrong?"

"Nothing!" Mom insisted. "Nothing at all!"

Ellie sank down in her seat, certain everyone was staring at her. The one who did lots of wrong things.

Ben spun a fork on the table. "What do you think is going on then? Why won't she talk to me?"

"She's probably embarrassed," replied Mom. "Remember what happened on our first date, Martin?"

Dad grinned. "How could I forget the burp that shook the world?"

That got Ellie and Ben interested.

"I was very nervous because your father was so handsome," said Mom as she buttered a slice of toast.

"Not to mention the only magician in the whole high school!" Dad added.

Mom hid behind her napkin. "Let's just say I drank my Coke too fast."

"After that earth-shattering belch, your mother ran out of the restaurant faster than a streak of lightning!" Dad laughed. "And she didn't talk to me for a whole week!"

"A week?" Ben whistled. "Geeze, Mom!"

"Well, I was mortified! But the cooler of Coke Mr. Romantic left on my porch won my heart," Mom

Chapter 18

patted Dad's hand.

"What did you expect?" Dad laughed. "I had to work my *looovvveee* magic!"

"TMI, Dad!" groaned Ben, rolling his eyes.

"I'm just saying that girls sometimes...have different perspectives than boys." Mom looked at Ben. "Give Sara a few days. She'll come around."

"In the meantime, young lady," Dad's eyes zoned in on Ellie again. "As your mother said, it's important that you apologize to Sara."

"Give her a picture from your nature notebook," Ben suggested. "Sara thinks you're an awesome artist just like we all do."

Of course her parents thought Ben's plan was great. But didn't anyone remember that Ellie *never ever* ripped pages out of her nature notebook?

"I'll get Ellie's pastels so she can write a nice message to Sara," said Mom.

"That would be sweet, El," said Ben as he pulled on his soccer cleats. "I'll drop it off on my way to the park."

A few minutes later, with her family watching, Ellie wrote *I'm sorry* and signed her name in her on-purpose-not-best handwriting using her pink pastel —the most boring color.

She *was* sorry. She was sorry for what she'd done. She was sorry her family was upset. She even felt sorry for making Sara cry a fox-colored tear.

But she was NOT sorry for saving Ben from being a Hawaii husband.

Chapter 19

A couple of days later, Ling and her parents came over with a bouquet to celebrate Dad's new job. His lunch meeting with Brent's uncle had gone better than expected, and in two weeks, he'd be an official magician with Kidz Parties & More.

"I didn't know you were going to do the paint thing," said Ling, joining Ellie under the weeping willow for the first time since the day of the dance.

"Me neither," whispered Ellie as she watched the jelly-bean shaped beetle she'd been drawing waddle into the grass. "Are you mad?"

"Kind of," said Ling as they headed to the raspberry bushes for a snack. "Was that a secret part of the plan or something?"

"No way, José!" Ellie told Ling she wanted to be prepared for a fox sighting. Then she tried to explain how the closer Sara's slimy, lip-glossy lips had gotten to Ben's, the better that smooth tube had felt in her hands.

"Oh, Ellie! Now I understand," Ling said. "Did you at least stop them before they kissed? You know...before they got to step four?"

Ellie chewed on her lip and shook her head no.

"Don't worry," Ling said, glancing over her shoulder at the parents who'd wandered from the picnic table on the deck to Mom's zinnia garden. "I have something to show you that will make everything okay." Then she pointed to the pocket of her polka-dotted dress.

"What?" Ellie gasped. "What is it?"

But Ling said the grown-ups were too close and she couldn't risk them seeing. While the girls waited for them to head back to the picnic table,

Chapter 19

Ling asked, "Did you wear the starfish dress to the dance?"

"No." Ellie popped a raspberry in her mouth. "A fish egg dress."

"Eww!" Ling wrinkled her nose. "That's almost as bad as my punishment. My parents are forcing me to wear my *regular* pink leotard to every ballet lesson this month!" Ling groaned.

"Oh no!" Ellie cried.

"They said covering for you while you were in the treehouse was the same as lying." Ling's shoulders slumped. "But they don't understand how totally *embarrassing* it is to wear a *regular* pink leotard! I'm the only babyish one in my ballet class because all the other girls have *plush* pink ones now!"

"I'm sorry," Ellie whispered. Her sorriness bubbled from her toes to her ears. Especially because Ling hadn't said, *See! I told you not to go in the treehouse!*

As the parents lingered by the zinnias, Ling

replied, "BFFs do stuff for each other regular friends wouldn't." Then she asked, "So, did your parents make you say sorry to Sara?"

After Ellie told Ling about the family meeting, Ling asked, "You didn't give her the Banana drawing, did you?"

"No way, José!" Ellie imagined her picture from the day of Banana's rescue. She'd even sketched the

banana peel (how he earned his name) that had been stuck on his head when Ellie tipped over the trash can to free him.

"Phew!" said Ling. "So, what did you give her?"

Ellie told her about the drawing she'd ripped from the front of her nature notebook where all her old sketches were. The ones from before Rachel had helped make her drawing fingers super strong.

"You really gave her a worm picture?" Ling

giggled.

"Yep!" Ellie grinned. Ben had said there'd been no answer at the McMillons' door, so he'd left it in the mailbox. Ellie liked imagining Sara screeching as she unfolded her drawing which looked more like a stretched-out wad of gum than a worm.

Ling flipped her braid over her shoulder as the parents lingered by the zinnias. "I know you're probably wondering, so I might as well just say it!"

"What?" Ellie asked, hoping it had something to do with the secret thing in her BFF's pocket.

"Eddy and Zhi didn't get engaged at the concert." Ling kicked at the grass with her glittery sandal. "But luckily Sophia had a plan to speed things up. I put an advertisement for engagement rings under the windshield wiper on Eddy's car."

"Why?" Ellie had no idea what Ling was talking about.

"Sophia says guys sometimes forget what the steps on the marriage list are," replied Ling. "The ad will remind Eddy to buy Zhi an engagement ring."

"Will Ben forget too?" Ellie asked hopefully as the parents finally settled at the picnic table.

"Maybe." Ling shrugged. "But Sara won't." Then she reached into the pocket of her dress and pulled out a tiny box wrapped in silver paper. *Ben* was written in pink magic marker across the top.

"What's that?" Ellie squeaked.

"Sara put it on your porch while I was getting the mail for Mom this morning," Ling said. "She didn't know I was watching, so I grabbed it as soon as she ran back to her house."

"It's not Ben's birthday!" Ellie protested.

"This isn't a birthday present," Ling hissed. "It's an engagement ring! It's the exact same size as the box in the advertisements!"

"Oh no!" Ellie dropped the raspberry she'd been

about to eat.

"Sophia says boys usually give the engagement rings, but sometimes a girl does if she's extra excited to get a Hawaii husband." Ling waved the box at Ellie. "Here, open it!"

"No way, José!" Ellie folded her arms.

"Don't you at least want to see how many karats it is?" Ling asked.

"Ben doesn't...like...carrots!" Flustered, Ellie reached for the box. Because now she had to see what a vegetable engagement ring looked like.

"Not that kind of carrot!" Ling said. "Sophia says the more karats an engagement ring has, the fancier it is. Besides, this is *good* news! I probably stopped Ben from becoming a Hawaii husband!"

Ling was right. This *was* good news! Without an engagement ring, Ben and Sara couldn't get married!

"Don't get too excited," warned Ling. "Ben could still buy one for Sara if they start talking again."

"I bet you girls are thirsty!"

Ellie and the Marriage List

Ellie whipped around to see Mom heading toward them holding two cups.

"Oh no!" squeaked Ling. "Grown-ups can't see the engagement ring!"

Ellie squeezed the tiny box so tightly that the paper seemed to burn her fingers. If she got in trouble, everyone would be angry with her again!

Ling leapt in front of Ellie, trying to block the engagement ring from view.

Clink! Clank! Clink! The ice in the cups Mom carried sounded louder than shattering glass.

"Quick!" Ling hissed. "Hide it!"

Then, because she didn't know what else to do, Ellie threw Ben's engagement ring into the raspberry bushes.

Chapter 20

That evening, they went to Scoops to celebrate Dad's magician job. Scoops was the best ice cream place in the world. The air smelled like sugary birthday parties and fun. Behind the counter, flavors of every color glimmered like jewels. But Ellie always got the same thing: an ice cream sundae with extra cherries.

"Are you sure that's enough for you, Ben?" Mom asked as they sat down. Ben had one scoop of vanilla without a drip-drop of chocolate or even a single sprinkle. Normally soccer made him eat like a dinosaur.

"Albert ordered pizza for the stockers." Ben shrugged. "I'm not hungry."

Ellie and the Marriage List

Mom took a sip of her strawberry milkshake. "Was Sara at work today?"

"She never works on Wednesdays," Ben said.

"What about Monday?" Mom asked.

"Please, Mom!" Ben grumbled. "Give it a rest!"

"Ben!" Dad used his warning voice. "Don't talk to your mother like that."

Chapter 20

But Ellie agreed with Ben. Scoops and Sara didn't mix!

"I told you guys." Ben sighed and pushed his bowl away. "Albert said she called in sick."

"This sounds like your first broken heart, son." Dad took a bite of his dark chocolate cone. "Lack of appetite is a classic symptom!"

A broken heart? That sounded serious. Ellie put her hand on her chest, relieved by the reassuring *thump, thump* beneath her T-shirt.

Ben rolled his eyes. "Geeze, I don't have a broken heart, Dad!"

"It's nothing to be ashamed of. I went through it with your mother after the burp that shook the world!"

"Maybe Sara thinks I ditched her," Ben said suddenly. "I mean, I did leave her standing there covered in paint." He balled up his napkin. "I was so worried about getting Ellie down, I didn't even bring her a towel or anything!"

"We were all pretty frantic that day," soothed Mom. "I'm sure Sara understood you were worried about your sister."

Ellie scooped a bite of sundae into her mouth, wondering how her family had already forgotten the no-Sara-talk-at-Scoops rule.

"How about some good news?" Dad asked, wiping his mouth and glancing at Mom.

"It's a surprise we hope you'll be excited about." Mom smiled at Ellie and Ben.

"What is it?" Ellie loved surprises!

Her parents exchanged a look before Dad said, "I'm going to build a magic workshop!"

"Go, Dad!" Ben grinned. "You're finally doing it!"

For years, Dad had talked about building a magic workshop. But it hadn't happened for so long, it sort of felt like it would keep on not happening.

"This job offer was just the nudge we needed to make the decision," Dad told them.

"Wow!" Ellie imagined a shimmery little hut with

Chapter 20

fireworks shooting out of the chimney.

"This transition will be a little
stressful for our family at first," Mom
continued. "But Brent's uncle's
company is extremely successful,
and he's certain that after your father
performs at a few parties, he'll gain a following."

"Then Martin the Magnificent will be booked
all over town!" Dad exclaimed. "But in the
meantime, I'll give magic lessons in my workshop to
supplement our income."

"I bet some guys from the soccer team would be
down for that," Ben said.

"Fantastic!" Dad clapped his hands. "When I
was a kid, my mentor magician had an amazing
workshop—it was the key to his success because he
used it for creation as well as teaching."

When Ellie asked what that meant, Dad said
he would also use the workshop for inventing new
magic tricks.

"This is the first real shot your father has to make his dream come true," said Mom. "We need to come together as a family to support him. Can we do that?"

"I'm in if Ellie is." Ben gave her a nudge.

"I'm in! I'm in!" Ellie couldn't wait to tell Ling and her AC friends.

But when Ben asked where the magic workshop would be, Dad had a sudden coughing attack and downed a cup of water. Then Mom knocked over her own cup trying to help.

After Dad recovered and the water had been mopped up, he finally answered Ben's question. "The magic workshop will go in the backyard." He said each word slowly, like he was testing them out.

"We'll have to take out my zinnia garden," Mom said quietly.

"And..." Dad coughed some more. "The weeping willow...will have to go too."

His words landed like a spaceship in the middle of

Chapter 20

the table. As Ellie looked at Ben, the only sound was a baby clanging her dad's keys in the next booth.

Ben must know what Mom and Dad were talking about. He understood these things better than she did.

But her brother looked just as mixed up as Ellie felt.

Chapter 21

"You mean, you're cutting down Ellie's tree?" Ben exploded. "Is that what you're saying?"

"Please lower your voice, son," said Dad, looking around.

"Just tell us! Are you cutting down Ellie's tree?" Ben did lower his voice a little, but this time his words were sharp, ripping through the ice-cream-scented air.

Mom swallowed a big swallow, then she said, "Yes. Yes, that's right."

"Your mother and I have arranged for two lumberjacks to do the job," Dad said. "They're well respected around town and—"

Chapter 21

"What's a lum...lum...lumberjack?" Ellie's tongue tripped over the sour-tasting word.

Glaring at Mom and Dad, Ben grumbled, "Lumberjacks are people who cut down trees."

Then Dad said something about the lumberjacks being twins. "Nic and Vic have a great reputation," he went on. "From what I hear they're very nice!"

"Nice people DON'T...cut down...trees!" Ellie cried. The thought of her beloved tree in danger made her whole body as shaky as the rope ladder.

"Ellie, sweetie," Mom said. "In all honesty, Dad and I had planned to have the weeping willow removed when we first moved in while I was pregnant with Ben."

"Even way back then, it was so big, it took over the yard. And it's dropping more leaves each year," added Dad.

But Ellie thought the soft, swingy leaves were beautiful when they were hanging from branches *or* scattered on the grass. And she was *proud* to have the most enormous tree in the neighborhood!

"But since the weeping willow came with the treehouse," Dad continued, "we decided to keep it around long enough for our kids to enjoy playing there."

"Now, after everything..." Mom bit her lip. "After everything that's happened, well..."

"It just makes most sense to cut down the tree," finished Dad.

"Maybe for you guys!" Ben crossed his arms. "But what about Ellie?"

As her parents tried to say stuff that made chopping down her tree okay, a storm began brewing inside Ellie.

You told us yourself you don't like the treehouse!

After what happened before the dance, this is the safest plan.

We'll go to the greenhouse and get a nice little cherry tree to plant on the other side of the yard.

But Ellie wasn't listening. Four awful words

Chapter 21

echoed louder and louder in her ears. Dad's words.

Cut down the tree.

Cut down the tree!

CUT DOWN THE TREE!

HER tree.

Ben looked at her. "You okay, El?"

"Don't...hurt...my...tree!" She pounded the table. Once. Twice. Three times!

"Oh, honey—" Mom started.

"Before you get upset, hear me out," Dad pleaded.

"NO WAY, JOSÉ!" Those three silly words had turned angrier and angrier since summer began.

The people with the key clanging baby were staring. Everyone in the whole place was. But Ellie didn't care.

Dad's eyes were shiny as he spoke to her. "You did such a great job at the AC dance. How would you like to be my official assistant? I have a hat and wand you can have. Just think, you can help me come up with the most magnificent trick yet in *our* workshop!"

Ellie and Ben's mouths hung open as Dad explained the worst part—how they'd use wood from the weeping willow to build his workshop.

"Isn't that special, Ellie?" Mom crooned. "Nothing goes to waste, and we still get to enjoy your tree. Just in a different way!" She pasted a smile on her face and reached for Ellie's hand.

But Ellie yanked it away, knocking her melted ice cream sundae soup onto the floor.

"You..." she stammered, glaring at her parents. "You... You're so *MEAN!*"

"That girl can't talk right!" laughed the key-clanging baby's older brother.

Ellie pushed up from the table with an angry shove. Her sneakers splashed in the ice cream sundae swamp below.

"And she certainly made a mess," said the lady working behind the counter.

Chapter 21

Ellie raced for the door, leaving behind a trail of gooey ice cream sundae footprints.

"Wait!" Ben was hot on her tail. "Ellie, hold up!"

She pulled on the door, but it was stuck! She

yanked harder, but it was no use. She was trapped just like in the treehouse window!

Behind her, Ben pushed the door instead. It swung open, and the warm evening air pulled them outside.

Ellie was crying so hard it felt like her whole body would fall apart. All she could hear were those four awful words.

CUT DOWN THE TREE!

Chapter 22

Ben took Ellie's hand and led her to a bench overlooking the Scoops parking lot.

Thawap, thawap, thawap went her sticky feet.

As they sat down, Mom and Dad rushed over.

"Please try to understand!" Mom reached to hug her, but for the first time ever, Ellie didn't let her. Instead, she imagined Banana darting around the backyard *trying to understand* where his home had gone or the bird rock band *trying to understand* why their stage wasn't where it had always been.

"Sweetheart." Dad knelt in front of her. "I know I'm the last person you want to talk to right now. But your mom and I love you so much and—"

"Go away!" Ellie had never spoken to Dad like that. But if her parents loved her, they wouldn't do this! Didn't they understand that her weeping willow wanted to be a tree? It wanted to rustle with creatures coming and going! It wanted to be Ellie's shady drawing place, NOT a magic workshop!

"Let me talk to Ellie alone, okay?" Ben said.

With her parents waiting in the car a moment later, Ben let Ellie sob. He let her sniffle and snort. He didn't even mind when she used his shoulder as a tissue.

"I can't believe it either, El," Ben said after a while. "That tree is super special to you. It's *your place.*"

"My *best* place." Tears splashed onto her legs.

"Parents can be clueless about what's important to kids. I mean, think about it. It's been like a zillion years since they were our age." He gave her a little smile.

But Ellie didn't have one smile left to give back. Not even for her brother.

Chapter 22

"I love that tree too," Ben continued. "I mean, what teenage guy says that, right?" He shrugged. "There's just something cool about it."

Ellie blinked at Ben through her smudged-up glasses, wishing Mom and Dad agreed.

"Here." Ben took off her glasses and cleaned them on his T-shirt. "These things look like they went over Niagara Falls." Then, gently, he put them back on her face.

Something about the way he did it made Ellie extra glad he was her brother. "I'm sorry, Ben!" she sniffled.

"For what?" he asked.

"For making you sad," Ellie whispered.

"Thanks, El," said Ben after a moment. "But I'm... okay."

But Ellie knew he wasn't. She'd seen his pulled-down mouth when there were no messages from Sara on his phone. She laid her head on her brother's shoulder and together they watched the sun dip behind the Scoops parking lot.

"If Mom and Dad are building the workshop so Dad can earn extra money, maybe I can give them what I earn at Albert's instead," Ben said. "I pretty much waste it all on junk food anyway."

"Really?" Ellie wiped at her wet cheeks.

"I'll talk to them," Ben said. "I'll try to change their minds."

Ellie felt like she had sprouted butterfly wings. No, eagle wings! "Do it now, okay?" she pleaded.

Ben shook his head. "Let's let things cool down. I'll catch them after soccer practice tomorrow."

Ellie popped up from the bench wondering if she might really soar away. She could wait if Ben said it was best. Keeping her tree safe was all that mattered.

Ben stood up too. "I'll do my best. I just can't promise anything."

But as Ellie hugged her brother, she knew he would do it. He'd make everything alright.

Ben could fix *anything*.

162

Chapter 23

The next morning, the girls stood on either side of the fence talking and eating raspberries. Ling was miserable because she was on her way to another ballet class in her regular pink leotard. But Ellie could barely contain her excitement when Ben walked through the gate between his morning soccer practice and his shift at Albert's.

"I talked to Mom and Dad about your tree before I left this morning," said Ben.

"You did?" Ellie bounced in the grass, glad she didn't have to wait for the good news.

Ben nodded. "While you were asleep. Before I left for soccer."

Ellie gave her brother a giant hug. "Thanks, Ben!"

"Don't thank me, El." He took a step back.

"What are you guys talking about?" Ling gave her regular pink leotard a grumpy tug.

Once Ben had explained the lumberjack situation, Ling cried, "Oh, Ellie! My regular pink leotard isn't the only emergency! Why didn't you tell me?"

Ellie was about to let Ling know that she *didn't* have an emergency because Ben had fixed it. But Ben spoke first. He said their parents had been in a good mood because of Dad's new job so he'd decided not to wait until after soccer. "I even made Mom coffee and brought Dad his *Magician Monthly* magazine to butter them up," he said.

Ellie waited for him to get to the part where her parents said, *Good idea, Ben! We'll keep the weeping willow forever!*

But he said something much worse.

"They still want to cut down your tree. I tried

everything." Ben sighed. "I'm sorry, El."

Ellie was desperate for her brother to smile. She longed for a *Just kidding!* Even a wink would be a relief. But Ben was serious. Super serious.

"I'll sell my regular pink leotards once my punishment is over!" Ling offered.

"That's cool of you, Ling," Ben said. "But they're not changing their minds. They wouldn't even take my pay from Albert's."

"They might!" insisted Ling. "Do you have anything to sell, Ellie?"

"My Banana drawing!" Ellie swallowed, imagining her favorite squirrel picture. Once, Grandma even called it a *masterpiece,* which she said meant very, very, very amazing and beautiful.

"Are you sure, Ellie?" Ling blinked at her. "It's your best one!"

"Stop!" Ben held up his hand. "It's no use, okay? There's nothing I can do. There's nothing *any of us* can do."

And that was the moment when Ellie understood that her tree *wasn't* safe. Knowing that made *her* feel unsafe too.

"The lumberjacks are coming next week," Ben said. "Mom and Dad told me this morning."

Ellie gulped, imagining giant hairy blobs with swords for teeth gnawing at her tree.

"I'm sorry, El." Ben picked up a soccer ball from the

grass and drop kicked it across the yard. "I did my best."

"Tree murderers!" Ling put her hands on her hips. "That's what those lumberjacks are!"

Ben shot her a look. "The drama isn't helping, Ling!"

"You have to try one more time!" Ling begged Ben. "Tell your parents this tree is Ellie's second best friend after me! Then they'll understand!"

Ben shook his head. "I've known Mom and Dad for fifteen years. Asking again will make things worse."

Ellie couldn't lose hope. Ben had fixed the broken tail on her piggy bank and found long lost remote controls. He knew how to make her dried up markers work again. Once he'd even convinced Mom to let them skip dinner and go straight to Scoops for dessert. If her brother could do all those things, he could do this too!

"One more time?" Ellie asked, gazing at her

favorite drawing place. Her favorite *everything* place.

Dad said the leaves scattered on the grass were messy. But Ellie saw a salad for caterpillars, a hiding place for ants, and the makings of future bird nests.

"I can't fix everything, guys," Ben said. "Look what happened with Sara. She still won't talk to me."

The girls exchanged a worried look as Ben trudged off to soccer practice.

Ellie had never seen her brother like this. *He* was the one who always cheered other people up. But now he needed her, and she didn't have one drop of cheerfulness left to give.

Chapter 24

That afternoon, Ling charged through Ellie's backyard gate like an angry lion.

"Worst ballet class ever!" she growled.

"What's wrong?" Ellie couldn't imagine anything worse than her terrible tree troubles.

"The marriage list is fake! Fake! Fake!" Ling shoved her sparkly sunglasses up on her nose. "It's the fakest thing in the whole world!"

Ellie set down her nature notebook and triangle pencil. This sounded like *good* news to her! "Are you sure?"

"Triple sure!" Ling huffed. "And I'm never speaking to Sophia again!"

Ellie and the Marriage List

Ellie gasped. "She's your BBF!"

"Not anymore she isn't!" Ling told Ellie that Sophia had met her in a dressing room before ballet class to give her a new *lucky* marriage list. "She said this list was special because it had a sticker from a real Hawaii pineapple by step six! She *promised* Zhi would move there by the end of the summer. But guess what?"

Before Ellie could answer, Ling screeched, "Sophia's a liar! A big liar!"

"Really?" Ellie leaned in close because she'd never heard Ling say one bad thing about Sophia.

"Yep!" Ling replied. "But it gets even worse because my mom *spied* on us! She came to tell us it was time for class, but she listened outside the dressing room door!" Ling cried. "Can you believe it? My *own mother!* Now she knows everything about the marriage list!"

"Oh no!" Ellie was glad *her* old

crumpled-up marriage list was stuffed under her pillow. Since Ling had found the engagement ring, she'd said Ellie didn't have to check it so much anymore.

"That's not all! Mom said none of it is true!" Ling groaned. "And she laughed at us! I was *mortified!*"

Ellie wrapped her BFF in a hug the same way Tara had done for her at the dance. "It's okay," she said. "Don't worry!"

Ling sniffled. "And Dad says teenagers aren't even *allowed* to get married because their parents are still in charge of them!"

"What about Ben and Sara?" Ellie asked hopefully.

"They can't get married either," Ling confirmed. "I'm happy for *you* about that part at least."

"Me too!" Ellie was happy enough to leap all the way up to the bird rock band stage!

"But I'm *crushed* for me!" Ling wailed. "The worst part is, Zhi thinks the whole thing is hilarious. Now she says she'll live at home forever just to torture me!"

But Ellie *wanted* to live with Ben forever. For now though, she just hoped things would go back to normal. Mom said summer soccer would be over soon. Then she and Ben could laugh at funny movies and eat too many Oreos again. They'd hike every day and look for foxes, only Ellie would have to draw them with her orange pastel since her fox-colored paint had ended up all over Sara.

"I just thought of something," said Ling suddenly. "If the marriage list isn't real, then what did you throw in the raspberry bushes? I mean, it can't be an engagement ring, can it?"

Ling was right. Ellie had no idea what was in that little box either! But she did know it was a present for her brother because it had his name on it! And since presents made people happy, Ellie took off for the raspberry bushes. "I'll find it!"

"Watch out for thorns!" Ling followed close

Chapter 24

behind.

Ellie dropped to the grass and scooted on her tummy until she'd wedged her head and shoulders into the tangle of poky branches.

"There it is!" called Ling, crouching next to Ellie.

"Where?" Ellie's glasses were crooked, so it was hard to see. And each time she tried to turn her head she got poked by prickers.

"This way!" Ling nudged Ellie's body to the right.

Ellie stretched further, pawing at the dirt and fallen berries. Finally, her fingers closed over the tiny box. She squeezed it tight, imagining her brother's

shiny smile when she handed it to him.

A few moments later, the girls burst through the back door. Ellie marched past Mom cutting vegetables for dinner and Dad who was organizing his travel magic bag.

"How about some lemonade, girls?" Mom asked. "I made a fresh pitcher."

Ling wanted some, but Ellie didn't have time for lemonade. She headed straight for her brother who was finishing off his own glass at the table.

"Here." She handed him the grimy present. "It's for you."

Ben squinted at the almost rubbed off *Ben* on the top. "What's this?"

"Did you make a gift for your brother, sweetie?" Dad looked up from the pile of color-changing scarves he was folding.

Ling stood next to Ellie and said, "She found it in the bushes."

"The bushes?" Mom raised her eyebrows. "You

mean the raspberry bushes?"

Ellie nodded, her heart pounding.

It was time. Time to say the hard part.

"It's from..." She took a deep breath. "It's from Sara."

Chapter 25

"*Sara?*" Mom, Dad, and Ben asked in unison.

"How did a present from Sara end up in the raspberry bushes?" Mom narrowed her eyes at Ellie.

"It certainly didn't walk in there on its own," said Dad.

Ellie stared at the gift in front of her brother. "Please open it," she whispered. Then he would be happy, and everyone would forget to be angry with her.

But Ben crossed his arms. "Not yet. I want to hear this too, El."

As she tried to explain what she'd done with Ben's gift, her family looked at her like she'd sprouted three heads.

"It's my fault!" Ling stepped forward. "I'm the one who saw Sara put the gift on the porch. I snuck over and took it."

Ellie couldn't let her BFF take all of the blame. "But I threw it!"

"What on earth has gotten into you girls?" Dad shook his head.

"I had to!" Ellie stomped her foot.

"Had to?" Ben glanced down at the dusty silver lump in front of him. "What do you mean *had to*?"

"She had to throw it in the bushes to stop the wedding!" Ling cried.

"Wedding?" Dad asked. "Who's getting married?"

"NOBODY!" Ellie cried.

"We *thought* Ben would turn into a Hawaii husband!" Ling explained.

"A *what*?" Ben looked like he was deciding if he should laugh or cry as he peeled away the silver paper. "Did you say *Hawaii husband*?"

"That's right!" Ling confirmed.

Suddenly, Mom started giggling. Giggling so hard she could barely get the words out. "Ling, does this have anything to do with that list your mother called me about?" Mom snorted. "The one with stickers and nail polish?"

"She told you too?" Ling groaned.

At the mention of stickers and nail polish, Ben turned his attention back to Sara's gift. Beneath the wrapping was a little velvet box. He popped it open and pulled out a folded paper before picking up what had been beneath it. "Whoa! This is awesome!" he breathed.

Ellie craned her neck to see. The tiny blue and yellow thing shining in Ben's hand was familiar. Very familiar. In fact, there was a mural of the same design in the AC lobby.

"A Down syndrome awareness pin!" Dad exclaimed.

Chapter 25

"How beautiful!" swooned Mom.

"I told Sara it would be cool to have one for my soccer uniform. I can't believe she remembered!" Ben stuck the pin near the brim of his hat so he wouldn't lose it before the next game.

Ling pointed to the paper in front of Ben. "What's that?" she asked.

Ben unfolded it and scanned the loopy handwriting. "Sara wrote a letter," he said softly.

Dad motioned everyone to his side of the table. "Come on, kids, give Ben some space."

First Ben read to himself. But then out loud for everyone to hear.

Dear Ben,

Tell Ellie I love her drawing so much that I hung it in my bedroom! Fun fact about me: I love worms! My family teases me because I rescue any I see stranded on the sidewalk. Now a not-so-fun-fact: I get embarrassed way too easily! And I'm the one who owes you guys an apology. I'm sorry for ghosting you. I should have laughed it off and gone to the dance as a clown fish or something! They're orange and white too, right?

Anyway, I was going to give you this pin at the dance. I even got a matching one! I wore it when we went out for Mom's birthday. I was so pumped when the waitress asked me about it!

I guess I should get to the point. I'm officially inviting you and Ellie to a (please-forgive-me-for-being-a-dork) picnic in my backyard after soccer practice tonight. This leads me to fun fact number two! I love to cook (I'm a work in progress though, so don't expect five-star cuisine yet!).

Sara xo

Chapter 25

"Let's go, Ben!" Ellie wanted to be at that picnic more than anything! Her I-want-to-be-Sara's-friend feelings raced back, stronger than ever. And knowing she'd actually *liked* the stretched-out-wad-of-gum worm drawing was a great surprise.

But Ling reminded Ellie she'd found the gift on her porch yesterday. "That means you can't go to the picnic. It was last night."

"Poor Sara probably worked hard preparing the food," Mom said.

"I bet she thinks you and Ben blew her off!" Ling was tearful. "All because of me! I should have minded my own business and just left the gift alone!"

"Yeah, you should have. But it is what it is now." Ben turned to Ellie. "So is this whole wedding list—"

"Marriage list!" Ling interrupted.

Ben rolled his eyes. "Okay, marriage list. Is this whole marriage list thing the reason you hid in the treehouse, El?"

Ellie nodded, staring at her sneakers. "Sorry, Ben."

Together the girls explained each of the six steps. Ellie hoped her family would finally understand why she'd been so worried.

But instead, they laughed. And laughed. And laughed.

"It might seem funny now that we know it's fake, but we thought Ben would be gone forever!" Ling said.

"FOREVER!" Ellie echoed, throwing her arms open wide to show just how long that was.

"You can't get rid of me that easily." Ben stood and stretched. "Someone has to keep you stocked with cheesy chips!" He motioned to a half empty bag on the counter.

Ben's words floated around Ellie like tiny, happy bubbles. In that moment, it felt like everything would be okay.

"What you did wasn't cool, El." He looped his arm

Chapter 25

over her shoulder. "But I forgive you. Besides, you know I've always got your back."

"Thanks, Ben." Ellie leaned on her brother with a happy sigh. A truly happy sigh.

"And guess what?" Ben asked as her parents and Ling watched.

"What?" Ellie looked up at her brother.

"I need you too."

"You do?" What could he possibly need *her* for?

"Totally." Ben nodded. "Nobody but you can cheer me up after we lose a big game." He gave the soccer ball on the floor a nudge with his toe. "And, of course, you're my go to for cool bug facts."

Ellie blinked, absorbing everything. Knowing Ben needed her too didn't just feel good. It felt amazing. Like she had an important job to do.

Ling looked at Ellie. "We'll fix stuff with Sara, right?"

"Right!" Ellie pumped her fist in the air. "Don't worry, Ben!"

She had to let Sara know how sorry she was. And she had to do it in a BIG way.

Because Ben needed her.

Chapter 26

The girls raced to Ellie's bedroom to work on a plan. But they had something important to do first. Ellie pulled the marriage list from beneath her pillow and ripped it up as Ling cheered. Together, they crammed every scrap into the jaws of Ellie's plastic T-Rex.

"What can we do to tell Sara we're sorry?" Ling asked just as Ellie spotted her jack-o-lantern bucket peeking out from beneath the bed. She grabbed it and began sifting through her leftover Halloween treats.

Ling flopped on Ellie's bed. "How can you be hungry at a time like this?"

"I'm not!" Ellie smiled.

"Then what are you doing?" Ling asked.

"A candy picnic!" Ellie exclaimed, waving her bucket. "For Sara!"

"Ooh, cool idea!" Ling said. "Zhi stole all my leftover Halloween candy, or I'd give you some too."

"That's okay!" Prickly with excitement, Ellie plucked a strawberry lollipop from her bucket. Sara loved strawberry things! She'd said so on the day of the hike!

As Ellie collected markers and paper for a candy menu, Ling touched the Christmas lights wrapped around Ellie's bedposts. "I remember when your dad put these up."

Ellie did too. The night after the girls spotted the ballerina ghost and they'd both been too terrified to sleep in their dark bedrooms.

As the girls talked, another idea began taking shape. An idea to make their picnic even more epic!

First, they made Ben promise not to text Sara

yet. Then, Ling ran home to change out of her
regular pink leotard and get the fairy lights Mr.
Yang had hung in her room. When she returned,
the girls draped them in the lowest branches of her
weeping willow along with Ellie's Christmas lights.
Even though they were bunched up in some spots
and barely visible between the shaggy-dog leaves in
others, Ellie thought the lights looked cool.

Ellie and the Marriage List

"It's beautiful out here!" Mom joined them as Ellie dumped candy on a blanket they'd laid below. "You girls are working hard."

Then Mom told them Dad had ordered dinner with a gift certificate Brent's uncle had given him as a welcome present for joining Kidz Parties & More.

"We thought pizza would be the perfect complement to a candy picnic!"

The girls squealed with excitement when Mom said she'd already phoned Mrs. Yang who agreed Ling could eat with them.

"This looks awesome!" Ben joined them. "Should I text Sara now?"

The girls agreed as Ellie put the finishing touches on the candy menu. They were ready. Really ready.

But Sara didn't respond to Ben's texts or calls. Even after the pizza came, the guest of honor was nowhere to be seen.

"Maybe she'll ignore us for eternity!" Ling said

as they trudged through Ellie's backyard gate after knocking on the McMillons' front door for the third time. Even though the pizza was almost gone, everyone had hoped Sara could at least enjoy her candy picnic.

But they didn't have time to wonder where she could be because Ben met them on the deck with the worst news ever. "The lumberjacks are coming!"

The word *lumberjack* made Ellie freeze in her tracks. With all the excitement, she'd almost forgotten about them.

"We know, Ben!" Ling rolled her eyes. "The tree murderers are coming next week. Which still gives us time to come up with a plan to stop their evil ways!"

"They're not coming next week." Ben swallowed. "They're coming in twenty minutes!" Ellie's heart sank as he told them the lumberjacks had texted Dad because they'd just gotten a cancellation nearby.

"They just want to see what equipment they need

and to talk prices and stuff." Ben tried to make Ellie feel better. "They won't cut down your tree tonight. You'll have time to say goodbye."

But Ellie didn't want to say goodbye. Not tonight. Not next week. Not ever!

She zipped across the yard with Ben and Ling hot on her tail. She had to turn off the lights. Those lumberjacks weren't allowed to see her tree all dressed up!

"I know!" Ling said. "Let's make signs to tell them not to hurt Ellie's tree! Remember the crabby old guy who used to live in Sara's house? He had *Keep Out* signs all over!"

"A protest might be better," said Ben. "But there's not enough time."

"What's that?" Ellie asked, choosing to focus on the *a protest might be better* part of what Ben said and not the *but there's not enough time* part.

"Remember when everyone protested Scoops ditching pumpkin ice cream after Halloween?" Ben

Chapter 26

asked. "It was supposed to be seasonal, but people went nuts over it!"

Ellie brightened at the memory of the pumpkin ice cream fans marching outside of Scoops waving signs and chanting, *I scream, you scream, we all scream for pumpkin ice cream!*

"Can we, Ben?" she begged, prickly with hope. "Please?"

"Sorry, El," said Ben. "The lumberjacks will be here any minute. Plus, we don't have signs."

Ellie blinked up at the wild branches of her weeping willow soaring into the orange and pink-streaked sky. Once Grandma had said that her tree looked like it had been plucked from a fairy tale. That was exactly how Ellie felt when she drew beneath it. Like she was nestled between the pages of a story brimming with wild creatures and leaf-swaying breezes. She couldn't give up. Not now.

With the memory of the Scoops protesters fresh in her mind, Ellie had an idea. She grabbed a slice of pizza from the almost-empty box and told the others to do the same. "Come on! Eat fast!"

As soon as the last crumb was gone, Ellie instructed Ben and Ling to use the markers from the candy menu to write on the insides of the empty boxes. After all, they were the perfect size for protest signs!

Chapter 26

"Epic idea!" Ben pulled the cap from the red marker.

"Yep," agreed Ling as she wiped her pizza box sign with a napkin. "A little greasy, but epic!"

Ben and Ling wrote: *Save Ellie's tree!* And Ellie drew a giant picture of Banana crying next to her weeping willow on the inside of her pizza box.

That's when the backyard gate opened.

Ellie leapt up and fiercely waved her pizza box sign. She opened her mouth to scream *Save my home!* at the lumberjacks.

To be Banana's voice.

To be every backyard creature's voice.

To be her tree's voice.

But there were no monstrous tree-chomping blobs galloping towards her.

When she saw who was coming instead, Ellie dropped her sign. Then she stumbled over to flip on the Christmas and fairy lights.

"Sara!" Ellie hissed to everyone. "Sara is here!"

Chapter 27

With Sara standing in front of them, nobody knew what to say.

For a moment, they all stood in silence beneath the shimmering branches. Then Sara reached to touch a strand of dangling lights. "Your tree looks pretty, Ellie," she said softly.

Feelings and words swirled from Ellie's toes to her ears. But this moment was so important, she didn't know which ones to choose. "Thanks," she managed.

"I got your message." Sara turned to Ben who looked as nervous as Ellie felt.

"Did you hear Ellie and me knocking on your door?" Ling asked.

Chapter 27

Sara shook her head and said, "I was at the movies."

"Really? The movies?" Ben's voice cracked. "Who'd you go with?"

Sara paused, smiling the tiniest smile. Then she said, "Mom and Dad."

"Oh. Okay." Ben grinned. "Cool."

Ellie couldn't wait another second. "I'm sorry!" She stared at Sara's freckles so she wouldn't have to see how mad the rest of her face was.

"For what?" Sara looked confused.

"For... For..." Ellie took a deep breath. "For everything!" *There!* Ellie hoped that covered all the bad things she'd done.

"You don't have anything to be sorry for, Ellie." Sara's voice wasn't angry. It was warm like Ellie's favorite hoodie.

"Yes, I do!" Ellie looked Sara right in the eye this time.

"Blame me!" Ling jumped in.

But Ellie wasn't done. "I made bad choices!" She repeated those words she'd heard from her parents over and over. "I squirted paint—"

But Sara cut her off. "I was the one who acted like a big baby. I took myself *way* too seriously." Her eyes flicked to Ben, then back to the girls. "I really am working on it, I promise." Then she gasped, eyeing Ben's hat. "Oh! Are you wearing the...?"

"It's the coolest gift I ever got. Way better than cookies from Albert's," Ben said. "Seriously. I love it. Thanks."

Sara barely nodded as she chewed on her bottom lip. "Then why didn't you guys come to my picnic?"

"Because of me!" Ellie cried.

"What do you mean?" Sara asked.

"I... I..." Ellie rubbed her sweaty palms on her T-shirt. "I threw it in the bushes!"

Sara took a step back. "You threw what in the

bushes?"

"Ben's gift," Ellie admitted. Suddenly she felt tired enough to curl up under the pizza boxes and go to sleep.

Ling stepped forward. "She was trying to save him!"

Sara scrunched up her eyebrows. "Save who?"

"Ben!" Ellie pointed at her brother.

"We thought she had to rescue him from becoming a Hawaii husband," Ling explained for the second time that day. "My former Best Ballet Friend gave me a fake marriage list."

"Did you say Hawaii husband?" Sara looked more confused than ever. "And what's a marriage list?"

By the time the whole story came out, Sara was laughing even harder than Ellie's family had. Ellie didn't think it was *that* funny, but at least Sara wasn't angry. The best part was when she hugged both girls and accepted their apologies.

"One problem with this whole Hawaii husband

idea is that neither of us has our driver's license yet."
Ben winked at Sara. "I guess I'll ride my bike to the
airport so I can catch my flight to Hawaii."

Sara put her hands on her hips. "Hey! Don't
forget your wife!"

"I have an old skateboard you can use,"
Ben teased. "I'll drag
you behind me."

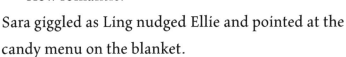

"How romantic!"
Sara giggled as Ling nudged Ellie and pointed at the
candy menu on the blanket.

Ellie scooped it up and handed it to Sara. "Here
you go!"

"Welcome to your candy picnic!" Ling held up
two lollipops. "Strawberry or grape?"

"Sara likes strawberry!" Ellie piped up.

"My very own candy picnic?" Sara looked excited.
"This is a first! And Ellie's right, I'm a major
strawberry fan!"

"It's to make up for Ben and Ellie missing yours,"

Chapter 27

said Ling.

"You totally didn't have to." Sara smiled at them. "But thanks, guys."

"Don't look at me!" Ben put an arm around Ellie and Ling's shoulders. "These two did all of the work."

That's when the gate opened once again. In the twilight, it was hard to see the four shadowy figures heading their way, but Ellie recognized her parents' voices.

"The lumberjacks!" Ling hissed, reaching for her sign. "The lumberjacks are here!"

Chapter 28

Ellie craned her neck, trying to see how sharp the lumberjacks' tree-chomping fangs were while Ben gave Sara a turbo speed version of the tree tragedy.

"Here!" Ling handed Ellie her sign as they approached.

"Kids, meet Nic and Vic," said Mom a moment later. "Nic and Vic meet the kids."

Dad cleared his throat, "They're the lumberjacks we told you about."

At first everyone was too shocked to speak. Nic and Vic weren't slimy or blobby. And there weren't sword-teeth hanging from their mouths. They just looked like nice ladies. Nice, matching ladies. In

Chapter 28

fact, the only way to tell them apart was that each wore a cap with her name on it. Everything else was identical. From their sandy ponytails to their boots and overalls.

"Wow!" exclaimed Vic, gazing up at the lights. "It's real pretty out here."

Ellie squeezed her sign so tightly that her fingers ached. "You have boy names," was all she could think to say.

"Ellie!" Mom cried. "That's rude, sweetie."

"Not rude at all," Nic laughed. "We surprise folks a lot. Our full names are Nicole and Victoria."

"But they're a little too girly for our taste!" said Vic with a grin.

"We use our nicknames in advertisements on purpose," explained Nic.

"Most people don't think women can cut down trees." Nic flexed her bowling ball-sized biceps. "That is until they meet us!"

Vic looked at everything spread beneath the tree.

"I sure hope we didn't break up a party."

Ellie waved her sign in the air. It was time to let the grown-ups know what was happening. "It's a proton!" she yelled.

"Protest," Ling whispered.

"It's a protest!" Ellie yelled. This time, the words sailed out of her mouth, clear and strong.

"A protest?" Dad looked from one kid to the next. "What's going on here?"

"This tree means a lot to us." Ben held out his sign too. "Especially to my little sister."

The grown-ups were quiet now, watching.

"Save Ellie's tree!" shouted Ben and Ling as Ellie stepped forward.

She thrust her sign in front of the grown-ups. "This is Banana."

Vic squinted at Ellie's drawing. "Is it just me, or does that banana have a tail?"

"He's a squirrel!" Ellie puffed out her chest. *The best squirrel in the whole world.*

Chapter 28

She almost pointed to her pizza box drawing again so they could see Banana's home. But instead, she whirled around to show them the real thing towering behind her.

"I saved Banana's life!" Now it was time to save his home. Her favorite squirrel's squeaks for help last summer echoed in her

head. She could still feel that giant, stinky trashcan against her palms as she tried to tip it over. It felt the same now. She was pushing against something bigger than herself. Much, much bigger.

At the sound of sniffling, Ellie spun around to see Dad hugging Mom and whispering in her ear.

Was Mom crying?

"You okay, mam?" asked Nic.

Mom nodded and wiped her eyes. "My allergies are acting up."

Chapter 28

"It's working!" Ben whispered to Ellie. "Keep going!"

Ling picked up Ellie's nature notebook and handed it to her. "My BFF is the best wildlife artist in the whole world!"

"A squirrel rescuer *and* a wildlife artist?" Vic let out a whistle. "Quite an accomplished young lady!"

Under the tangled Christmas and fairy lights, Ellie showed everyone the drawings in her nature notebook. There was the fat robin she hoped had a belly full of babies, the shiny-as-a-jellybean beetle, and, of course, Banana, along with one of his best chipmunk friends.

Mom's voice quivered. "Is that the one you said likes racing with Banana?"

Ellie nodded. "My tree is good for racing!"

Sara smiled at her and held out something round. "And for making new friends." *That's why she'd been so quiet!* Sara had been making her own paper plate *Save Ellie's Tree* sign.

"And drawing!" Ellie hugged her nature notebook and stood next to Sara. Freckles or not, Sara *was* her friend now. After all, only a real friend would help her do something this important.

"And ballet!" Ling circled her hands above her head and twirled beneath the lights.

Love for her tree overflowed inside of Ellie. Stretching her arms out wide, she hugged the elephant-sized trunk with all her might.

"Ellie, sweetie," Mom said. "Come here. Your father and I want to talk to you."

"No way, José!" Ellie squeezed tighter.

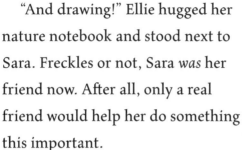

Chapter 28

She knew she was supposed to be extra good after the bad things she'd done. But how could she? How could she when her tree couldn't say no to the lumberjacks?

The animals and insects couldn't say no either.

But Ellie could.

Chapter 29

By now, the moon, white as a giant snowball, had climbed high in the sky, and crickets were chirping from every corner of the yard.

"I'm sorry for wasting your time, ladies," Dad said to Nic and Vic. "But I've made a terrible mistake."

"We both have!" Mom's eyes were shiny as she spoke. "This job change will be an adjustment. But that doesn't give us the right to strip away part of our family."

"An important part of our family," Dad added, looking at Ellie. "The weeping willow is here to stay."

Ellie's mind raced and her heart thumped.

Chapter 29

"Forever?"

"Forever," her parents answered.

"Did you hear that?" Ben picked Ellie up and swung her around. "You did it! You rescued your tree!"

She was scared to believe it. But she was more scared *not* to believe it. So, she tipped her head back and shouted into the sleepy branches above. "You're safe! You're safe!"

In the end, Nic and Vic agreed to tear down the treehouse if Dad put on a magic show at Nic's son's party. Not only that, but Nic and Vic liked Ellie's sign so much, they offered to build a squirrel nest box for Banana and his friends to put in its place.

Ellie floated around the group, hugging everyone—even Nic and Vic.

Vic looked at Nic. "I don't know about you, but this is one job I'm glad to walk away from."

Nic nodded and wiped her eyes. "I'm right there with you, sis. A tree as loved as this one deserves its place in the backyard."

After they left, everyone else worked together to clean up the remains of the protest and the candy picnic.

As Ellie picked up her markers, a firefly blinked in and out of the shadowy leaves. It was so cute, she wanted to remember every bit of its teensy body so she could draw it in her nature notebook tomorrow.

"Since you aren't building the workshop, maybe you can give magic lessons online, Dad," Ben suggested as everyone tossed paper plates and candy wrappers into a garbage bag.

"I don't think so. Magic is a hands-on experience, son," Dad said. "Even if I have to pick up a few hours at the office, we'll make do somehow."

But Ellie didn't want her dad to go back to that boring office job ever again. It sounded even worse than her pink basement playroom dusting job!

Chapter 29

That was it!

Dad could turn her boring playroom into a magic workshop! Since she never played there, he could make it any color he wanted!

"That's quite a generous offer," said Dad after she'd explained. "Are you sure, honey?"

"She's sure!" Ling said. "Ellie would rather go to the dentist than hang out in her playroom!"

"I don't blame you," Sara said to Ellie. "I'm an outside kind of girl too!"

As everyone discussed her idea, Ellie thought about her weeping willow. Soon it would be free to stretch its branches, and the ballerina ghost would have to find a new place to dance at midnight!

When it was time for Sara to go home, Ben offered to walk her back across the street.

"How about just to the gate?" Sara glanced at Ellie. "You should hang here. We've got a full shift at Albert's tomorrow to catch up."

A few moments later, Ling pointed at Ben and

Sara lingering by the backyard gate. "I bet they're kissing!" she whispered.

It was too dark for Ellie to see, but even if they were, she didn't mind. Because at this moment, every person, creature, and tree she loved was happy.

At least they *were*, until Ling let out the most blood-curdling scream Ellie had ever heard.

Chapter 30

With a shaking finger, Ling pointed into the branches above. Then Ellie saw. She saw exactly what was freaking Ling out.

Now, Ellie was freaking out too. She opened her mouth and let out a shriek so loud it seemed to bounce off the stars.

There, in the window of the treehouse, was that same glowing thing they'd seen at that long-ago sleepover. Only now, standing directly beneath the treehouse, with her glasses on, Ellie could see it better.

Much better.

"It's midnight!" Ling shrieked. "It must be

midnight! Remember what the Ghost Guru said?"

"It's not even close to midnight," said Ben. "Did you say *ghost guru*?"

The girls clung to each other, too terrified to explain.

"Girls!" Dad said. "Please calm down!"

"But the ballerina ghost is probably putting a spell on us at this very moment!" Ling squeaked.

Mom stepped in too. "We've had such a beautiful night, don't ruin it with—"

"She's there!" Ellie pointed. "See her?"

"Come on, El," Ben groaned. "Not again!"

Chapter 30

"Wait a minute, son!" Dad took a few steps towards the treehouse. "The girls are right. There *is* something up there!"

That's when Ben and Mom gasped. They saw it too! *Finally! Her family believed them!*

Like a fearless lion, Ben marched even closer to the treehouse. That's when Ellie noticed something strange about the ballerina ghost.

"She's not... She's not..."

"What, sweetie?" Mom asked. "What are you trying to say?"

"Dancing!" Ellie shouted. The ballerina ghost hadn't moved one teeny bit!

"Ellie's right!" Ling shrieked. "Maybe she's too busy morphing us into toads!"

But the more Ellie looked at the thing in the window, the less it looked like a ballerina ghost. In fact, that round, white thing was beginning to look quite familiar.

"What do you want from me, ballerina ghost?"

Ling shouted. "Is it my plush pink leotard? Is that it?"

Relief washed over Ellie. She knew exactly what was in the treehouse window! And it wasn't scary at all! "The ballerina ghost isn't real!" The sentence flew out of her mouth so quickly, it sounded more like one long, bouncy, excited word.

"Did you say what I think you said?" Ling shrieked. "Did you say the ballerina ghost isn't real?"

"Yep!" *The ballerina ghost is just as fake as the marriage list!*

"But she's staring right at me!" Ling's voice quivered.

"Look!" Ellie untangled herself from her BFF's grasp and pointed. "It's the moon!"

"Ellie's right," exclaimed Dad. "It's only a reflection in the treehouse window!"

Mom kissed Ellie's head. "You just solved your very own mystery."

"It's only the moon. It's only the moon. It's only

the moon," Ling repeated. "Oh Ellie, thank goodness
you figured it out! I thought I'd have to give up my
plush pink leotard just to get rid of the ballerina
ghost!"

"Ling!" Zhi's voice rang out from next door.
"Mom says you have to get home *now!*"

Ling turned to Ellie and grumbled, "The only bad
part about all of this is that I'll never have a walk-in
closet!"

"Yes, you will!" Ellie reminded Ling she'd have her own *everything* when she was a movie star.

That made Ling smile. But she wasn't the only one. Her whole family was happy and smiling beneath the blinking lights above.

Ellie felt like a whole new girl. A powerful girl. A girl who could do amazing things. After all, she'd done something even Ben couldn't do. She'd rescued her tree! And that wasn't all. She'd climbed a wobbly rope ladder into the creepiest treehouse in the world, planned a candy picnic, and organized a protest. Not to mention, she'd solved the ballerina ghost mystery and made a friend with freckles. Plus, she'd given Dad his very own magic workshop!

Chapter 30

In the branches above, there was a skittering of feet. Maybe it was Banana. Maybe it was one of his friends. Whoever it was, it had a home. A forever home.

Before heading in for the night, Ellie stood at her back door looking out into her sleepy backyard. "Goodnight!" she waved to her tree. Then came the best words ever. "See you tomorrow!"

The weeping willow seemed to wave back, swaying between the stars and the moon.

Just then, a flicker caught her eye. It was that same playful firefly she'd seen earlier! It must have followed her across the yard. The tiny insect circled, dove, and swooped before flying off into the night.

One extra sparkle in the darkness.

THE END

Down Syndrome is my Superpower!
A few facts about DS

What is a chromosome?

Even though Ellie thinks talking about chromosomes is boring, they're a big part of her story. Most of us have 46 of these teeny thread-like structures in each of our body's cells. Chromosomes carry important information about who we are and how our bodies work.

What is Down syndrome?

Children with Down syndrome have an extra full (or partial) chromosome in all or some of their cells. Although this genetic difference often leads to learning and physical challenges, people with DS are capable of awesome things from going to college to running marathons. In fact, Ellie's family gave her an extra sparkle ring in celebration of her 47th chromosome.

Why do Ellie's muscles sometimes feel like wobbly spaghetti noodles?

Like many children who have Down syndrome, Ellie has a condition called hypotonia or low muscle tone. Hypotonia can make it more difficult (but certainly not impossible!) to do things like hula hooping, rescuing squirrels, and climbing rope ladders.

Are all people with Down syndrome alike?

As Ellie would say, *No way, José!* Each child with Down syndrome has his or her own unique strengths, challenges, and dreams, just like other kids.

What is occupational therapy?

Occupational therapists guide kids with Down syndrome to become more independent in performing everyday activities such as shoe tying, packing school lunches, and undertaking hobbies like drawing. But that's not all. OTs help with lots of things from sensory to social interventions. In fact, one of the most important people in Ellie's journey to become a wildlife artist is her occupational therapist, Rachel, who teaches her lots of cool exercises to strengthen her hands and fingers.

What is speech therapy?

Because people with Down syndrome usually face some degree of difficulty with language, speech therapists have an important job to do. Not only do they help kids like Ellie learn to communicate more clearly, but they are also qualified to teach techniques in areas such as feeding, eating and cognition. Ellie feels especially lucky to have her speech therapist, Maria, who rewards her with cool bug stickers for all of her hard work.

What is physical therapy?

Strength, coordination, and balance are just some

of the ways physical therapists help kids with Down syndrome. Ellie likes remembering the fun things she did with her physical therapist, Neema, at the park. Some of her favorite activities were playing pirates on the bouncy bridge and carrying rocks up and down the play structure stairs.

If you'd like to learn more about Down syndrome, you can visit the website of the National Down Syndrome Society (NDSS) at https://ndss.org/.

Acknowledgements

First off, a weeping-willow-sized thank you to the diversity-focused founder of Lantana Publishing, Alice Curry.

I'd be lost without Katrina Gutierrez's editorial guidance and insight as a parent of a child with Down syndrome. To her sweet daughter, Sinta—

never stop dancing!

I'm beyond grateful to therapists Hosanna Say Camacho and Dos de Jesus as well as to the Aventajado, Frazzetta, and Antiojo families for sharing their experiences and reading early drafts.

I loved volunteering with the Down syndrome community through Gigi's Playhouse, especially connecting with my friend, Joe Pawsey.

To my rock star illustrator, Lucy Rogers, you exceeded every expectation!

A big shout out to editor, Kathy Webb, cover designer, Jenny Stephenson, and typesetter, Emily Bornoff.

I'm thankful for my friends' and entire family's unwavering support—especially the best first readers ever: my mom and my sons, Carson, Travis, Chase, and Preston.

Above all, this book wouldn't be possible without God's love. Because of the people He's blessed me with, Ellie's story can truly sparkle.